Dragon Tree

League of the DragonTree

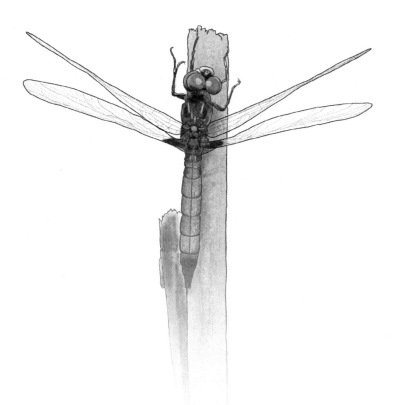

Shon M. Shaffer

Illustrated by Bren Shaffer

Printed in the United States of America

This book is a work of fiction. Any references to real people, events, establishments, organizations, or locales are intended solely to provide a sense of authenticity and are used fictitiously. All other characters, incidents, and dialogue are drawn from the author's imagination and are not to be construed as real.

Cover art created by Bren Shaffer

This is for my wife who personifies the best qualities I tried to convey through the main characters. Also for Larry Evans, the quintessential encourager and wonderful goad. He is remembered lovingly and missed greatly. And lastly for my new-old, big brother John, we finally get to see how our own adventure plays out after 46 years in-waiting.

DragonTree

Acknowledgments

Bren, your art elevates everything it graces. Thanks for the beautiful contributions and for bringing visual life to the story.

Billi Jo, thanks for slogging through the mire and offering invaluable insight, patient editing and most of all the abundant love and friendship.

D & J Lewis, for understanding how to communicate grace and so many of its nuances.
To GOD in whom all things are possible; His world is a fearful and wonderful place and not least of all interesting.

A special thanks goes to Craig Schenning for being the first to take a chance on the DragonTree series.

Preface

I've taken extreme liberties with the longevity, time-lines, creature behavior and pretty much every element in the book relating to the main characters. That is and was done for convenience sake, reality casts a very cold blanket over warm ideas. How could I have main characters that only live for a few months? Just a year? The answers are simple...ignore realism, the rest will follow.

I figured that once I got past the conceit of talking insects, worrying about details that only an Odonatist, an Apiarist or even a Lepidopterist would bludgeon me over was pointless. I hope at the very least to remain consistent with longevity, behavior and lifetimes I've settled upon for the entire story cycle. Please, just ignore the elastic reality that encompasses the world of DragonTree and it's all too common critters. I hope most of all, that I've been able to convey, the elements of each species that first captivated my imagination. In the end, this whole exercise may be little more than the consequences of spending far too much time under the blazing sun, much of which took place in staggeringly noisome swampland.

So, shrug off the safe precepts of the known entomological world and enter one in which the bugs can talk, play games and most importantly, realize the true cost of freedom.

Contents

Chapter One

Watchers

The shimmering surface of the Fen rippled. The menacing creatures hidden deep in the shadows of the trees that grew along the western shore reacted.

Another one...

A small brown form emerged from the center of the ripples and crawled its way upward, seeking the warmth of the brilliant morning sunlight. The watchers in the shadows grew more agitated. They were eager to act. Their black and yellow bodies quivered with excitement. The largest of their number held them in place with a firm and unspoken command.

Not yet...

They heard her with their minds and obeyed without question. They kept themselves hidden and watched as the newly emerged creature began to change. Its brown shell slowly split open revealing a light blue form with four diaphanous wings.

They watched as it darted all about the body of water that had captivated their attention for days on end. They watched as it soared high and then angled low to skim the water's surface, avoiding a predatory death by the slimmest margin. They watched as it streaked straight away and disappeared into the shadow of the one prominent tree on the western shore.

We have seen enough, it is time to return...

The large bee hovered about and flew away from the Fen, the rest followed. She was known only as Second, and she would lead the others back to Hive, back to their Queen. When they arrived, Second would give report of all they had seen. Her warrior-drones formed a protective ring around her, they kept to the shadows and flew north into the great swamp. Deep within its hidden fastness, unseen by other creatures, they would begin to make their steady way eastward.

As they traveled, their Queen's Imperative pulsed through their shared mind.

We are Legion...We are Hive...We shall conquer....

Nymph

Chapter Two

Firsts

"Flying! I'm really flying!" Tuss shouted as he increased speed and gained altitude. He was overcome with excitement. He was using his new wings for the very first time. That excitement increased when he realized that he'd just used his new voice for the first time too.

Oh! He thought, *I guess everything I do for a while will be a first.*

He was a young Blue Dasher dragonfly finally free from the constraining protective shell. He'd waited the entire morning, which seemed endless, clinging to the reed as the sun's warmth worked the miraculous changes.

Actually, Tuss thought, *I've been waiting my entire life for this, not just this morning.* That was true but he also knew that his entire life wasn't all that long, twenty-four phases of the moon and all of them until now, spent underwater as a dragonfly nymph. It only felt like a long time, *far too long*, knowing he was meant to fly but having to wait until the right time, which had finally arrived. He was flying.

He whooped with joy and streaked across the surface of the Fen. He saw the blue of the sky mirrored below him, the clouds reflected in the water wavered and danced. He pulled up and spun about in a soaring spiral which made him dizzy. He realized then that he wasn't ready for such a complex maneuver, *not yet, but I will be soon enough!*

The swish of wings followed by a sharp cry startled him. His heart jumped as a large black shadow flashed over him. *A bird? Is that what they're really like?*

It was a bird, sleek, black and deadly looking, something he needed to avoid. He was also thinking that it was very beautiful too. He hovered for a moment admiring the strength those large wings must give it, until he realized, *Oh! Oh no! It's not just a bird; it's a bird that thinks I'm its next meal!*

Tuss, nearly overcome with the horror of what had almost happened, didn't linger any longer. He didn't need to see if it would turn and come back for him, it was time to move. Motivated by a fear, not unlike the feeling he'd had when fleeing from a large fish, he put his amazing new wings in motion, veered sharply downwards, diving as fast as they would propel him. It was necessary to get closer to the Fen's surface as quickly as he could.

Didn't I learn anything in class, from the many warnings? The Teachers had scolded him many times about his daydreaming. It was one of his bad habits and he'd endured not just the scoldings but the teasing of his friends too. They'd catch him, lost in his thoughts and often do something to scare him back into the present, much like the bird that'd just about had him for breakfast.

I'm even doing it now, instead of focusing on this new world with all its wonder; the new sights, smells and sounds! And worst of all, I was nearly eaten on my very first day in the air because of it!

He wanted to promise himself that he'd stop forthwith, but he knew better. He was who he was and had learned to accept the good with the bad, *it's part of who I am. The rest of me, what I'm going to be in this new life, is yet to be discovered.*

He steepened his angle and poured on speed. He only pulled up from the dangerous dive and flattened his trajectory when he was just a few wing-beats from the water's glittering surface. The rush of speed and excitement overwhelmed his senses. He was filled again with the thrill of flying. The freedom his new wings provided him was greater than he'd ever imagined.

"Just don't die from foolishness Tussilago," he shouted out, hoping that the sound of his voice would further drive the point home. "You've a future to look forward to after all! But only if you keep your wits long enough to see it."

He focused upwards, the feathery beast was gone, the lessons were correct about the predatory birds, *at least that one.* They don't always pursue their prey close to the Fen's surface. *No more lapses,* he promised himself. Tuss knew that he needed to learn from the mistake and fly forward to what's next. But what was next and did he really want to face it?

They'd learned that solitude and a peaceful life, one spent in isolation, was next. Everything within Tuss rebelled against the very idea. This new world, the one of fresh air and bright sunlight, was filled with the promise of endless possibilities. How could he experience all of it alone, as the dragonfly Tradition suggested? In isolation?

The newfound freedom of flying, amazing as it was, couldn't overcome the depression that filled his heart right then. He wasn't meant to be alone. Memories of months spent in the cool, watery dark of the Fen's depths flooded him. Tuss would've gone mad down there if it weren't for the companionship of his friends. They spent every free moment together.

And to think that the change from then to now happened only just this morning. It felt like he was dying inside, or at least part of him felt that way. *Does change always have to feel like this?* He asked himself, already knowing the answer, *in some way, yes, change does feel that way, but not always, what sometimes happens is amazing!*

He wondered what his friends, could he call them that any longer, were going through right now? Were they feeling the same way? Was it this confusing for them?

This was a day unlike any he'd ever lived before; changes, one upon another, and so many of them as painful as they are exciting. *This is a lot like it was when I first became aware of who I was. A newly hatched nymph, my mind filled with awe and wonder, surrounded by a strange world I couldn't begin to understand. There was the call. Then came the classes, the lectures and the Tradition. Then, best of all, I met my friends and from that point on, everything began to make sense, but before that...*

***

The first time Tuss heard the strange thrumming vibrate through the water he hid in fear. It repeated over and over, teasing his awakening mind with its familiarity until he realized that he could actually understand it and that it was calling to him. He had no idea how it knew he was there, in the cold dark depths, or even who he was, all of which was all right, because, he hardly knew himself. And where was here?

The sound, at first a fearful thing, had gradually become comforting and compelling. Something deep within him responded to it. Tussilago, soon to be called Tuss, left his shelter and searched for the source. What he found was other nymphs, the upper reaches of his watery world and the blurry reality of what he'd transform into, an adult dragonfly. The time of learning began then; that period of his life would last for twenty-four moon phases. All the while he never stopped wondering if he would one day find the source of that first thrumming voice that called to him and beckoned him to rise up and seek the light.

***

The Teachers and Elders spoke to them from above as they listened from the shallows. The sound of their voices was muffled and odd, much like the original call that drew them so soon after their hatching. Tuss had been the first to answer. Cas, and Coria came next, followed closely by dozens of others. Briza was the last to arrive, complaining that; *"if someone had informed me sooner, I would've come sooner!"* His was the first underwater voice Tuss had heard. Cas' was the second. Hers was much nicer sounding, except for the fact that she was telling the noisy miscreant Briza, to be quite long enough for her to hear what was being said from above.

That was how he met them, Briza, the wildest member of their hatching, the one most likely to cause trouble and Cas, whom he'd eventually consider to be his closest friend. Briza was the first Tuss made friends with, though the relationship was more a case of Tuss being the only nymph patient enough to tolerate his antics than anything else. So, by default they were friends. The trouble was that no one besides Cas would hang out with the pair. Briza was that off-putting. And she only did so because of her natural affinity for Tuss' kind nature. Eventually Briza learned to control his impulses making it possible for the trio to expand their friendship and include Aneth, Leon, Coria, Mira, Ace and Gal. The nine became friends, and in a short matter of time, would become inseparable.

***

Thinking about those times before, below the surface surrounded by his friends, stuck in classes and the endless lectures about Tradition and independence deepened Tuss' sense of loss. Sadness filled him as he thought about how different life would be now that he'd emerged. It was time to put friends and games behind him. It was time to be a dragonfly. He could even hear the voice of the Elder Salix saying, "and once emerged you will find your own area of the Fen. You will patrol there, hawk there, and exert your control there. It's where your life will be spent. You will live out your days in independence and solitude."

"Why patrol?" Someone would ask.

The answer was always a variation on the same theme; "Danger is everywhere, birds, spiders, frogs, and so forth. Only by patrolling may we know when dangers are present." There was never any *real* explanation about what they should do if said dangers were actually detected. And that always struck Tuss as an odd, if not extremely important oversight.

And then the other questions, those that bothered him the most followed, he'd asked them himself on more than one occasion, "Why solitude? Why isolation?"

And like the question about danger, when asked why it was so, why life had to be lived in solitude? The unsatisfying answer was always the same, "because that's what makes us what we are, it's the nature of our kind. You are dragonflies, therefore...the rest ran together into a nonsensical *blah-blah-blah*.

So in the end, he and his classmates had to satisfy themselves with incomplete responses, gaps in stories and lots of speculation about what life might be like once they emerged. The Teachers, usually one of the three Elders, taught the classes. On rare occasions some other dragonfly would fill in. Regardless of who was speaking, the nymphs listened wearily as seemingly innumerable days of mind numbing boredom flowed past, one after another.

The subject of *hawking* at least was interesting and a clear enough doctrine. Below, the nymphs called hawking which was what was done above the surface, hunting. It's how they ate and dragonfly nymphs were nothing if not voracious eaters, fierce competitors and fearfully successful hunters. Tuss knew he'd miss the thrill of the underwater hunt. They went after almost anything, primarily unintelligent water insects, though when they packed together, they could overcome surprisingly large sized minnows. And that was the best of times, hunting with his friends. Even back then he hated the idea of the impending changes, knowing the days of being surrounded by close companions would end. No more sneaking off to play games that filled the time with fun and laughter. All of that closeness would come to a tragic end as life forced changes upon them. He consoled himself with the reminder that, "You want to emerge! You want to transform into what you're meant to be, and most of all Tussilago, you want to fly and discover what true freedom is!"

***

And just like that, Tuss' time of reverie was over. The inevitable changes had happened, the old life had passed away the new had begun. He had no choice but to come to terms with what it all meant. "It isn't right!" He shouted again. "What am I supposed to do to pass the time if I'm not allowed to be with my friends?" Shouting aloud what had been pent up inside was a great relief. It helped him calm down and once again forced the depressing thoughts to the back of his mind. When they were banished, his focus turned outward.

"Oh yeah!" Tuss said as he looked all about, realizing that he'd been hovering while daydreaming of the past. He felt the easy beat of his wings and the unbelievable lightness of his frame. He saw the world of air, still so new to him, spread in every direction, all of it an opportunity for adventure except, *I can't go too high, that's too dangerous. And I'm just above the surface, so no going down, but everywhere else...*

He chose a direction opposite from that of the bird he'd had the near miss with and streaked away.

"I'm flying, I'm really flying!" He shouted with renewed joy as he raced down the wind, laughing at himself for dwelling on the past when he could enjoy the future, which was right now. Everywhere he looked, there was something fresh to grab his attention. He reveled at the newness of it all.

Life can be so surprising! Tuss streaked through the shrubby trees on the west bank of the Fen. *Just when I think I've figured something out or I think I'm doing exactly what I want, something new comes along and changes my perspective.* He spun northwards and streaked over the thicket of reeds that separated the north end of the Fen from the great swamp. *Yeah, it sure looks like whatever lies ahead, will be interesting, hopefully not too lonely, but most definitely, it'll be interesting.* He slowed as a strange coldness washed over him. It wasn't caused by the air or a cloud shadow, but by something he couldn't identify. It was akin to fear, not quite the same as when he realized that he'd almost been eaten. It was close enough though. He stopped and surveyed the surroundings. His new eyes, so much better than the old, could take in almost more information than his young mind could process. Nothing he saw accounted for the sense of chilly dread that'd stopped him short, *I don't see anything but I'll be extra careful all the same; I don't want to be too relaxed. No more close calls with birds or otherwise today.*

He turned south and sped towards the great tree that grew on the western shore, the one his kind called the DragonTree. The odd feeling of cold began to diminish and with it his attentiveness to his surroundings.

"Wow! The Tree is amazing from up here. This is nothing like seeing it from below!" He chided himself for not flying to it first. How could he ignore the awe inspiring central figure in so much of his folk's history, not to mention the most prominent landmark of the entire Fen?

The questions were scarcely formed in his head, when a deep rumbling voice startled him.

"WATCH OUT!"

Chapter Three

A New Friend

"WHOA!" Tuss shouted even as he reacted to the booming sound. The looming presence that shouted the warning was directly ahead. He folded his wings and dropped towards the water's surface, spun about in a twisting spiral. Too late he realized that such a maneuver was way too complicated for him, so new to flying.

Tuss almost got away with it anyway, almost.

He'd avoided the large, deep-voiced presence but was unable to avoid skimming the Fen's surface with one of his wings. The contact, slight as it was, forced him to adjust his direction. A large tree branch seemed to appear from nowhere and that complicated his predicament further by blocking his way. He had to turn sharply again to avoid certain disaster. He reflexively barrel-rolled, having no other choice, the entire time knowing it too, was beyond his skill level. He also knew that a collision would end his first day as a flier in the worst way possible.

The hard turn kept him from crashing headlong into the thick branch but aimed him directly at a large patch of tall reeds. He steered for the most open course through them, closed his eyes and hoped for the best. Miraculously he missed flying straight into anything sturdy enough to knock him senseless, though his wings took a slight battering. The reeds were springy but tough. Dragonfly wings, particularity new dragonfly wings are fragile, but thankfully flexible. All four made it-through a little worse for the wear but uninjured.

Tuss' wild flight finally came to an end when he passed through the last of the obstructions and ended not so gently in a soft patch of tall springy grass. After the momentary shock wore off, he checked himself thoroughly, marveling over the fact that he'd avoided hurting himself badly. He was grateful, his future could've been unalterably changed and not for the good. Broken winged dragonflies lived unhappy and most usually, short lives.

He pulled free from the entanglement, which took all six of his tarsi. The grass around him was an intertwined mess. He even needed to use his clasper once, which also being new, felt very awkward. As he emerged from the plight that his inattention had gotten him into, he pondered whether or not it would even be possible to ever feel right in this strange new form.

Once he was clear and able to hover he took stock, *Okay, my wings are working fine. Nothing's hurt and aside from feeling foolish, I guess I'm all right.*

He chided himself, already forgetting why he'd changed course so abruptly. "Well Tuss, you clumsy oaf, what'd you expect on your first day?" He swooped back through the reeds, ducked under the branch that he'd almost brained himself on and flew back out to the open water. The unplanned detour happily behind him, he sighed aloud, "well, I shouldn't be so hard on myself, I only just began to fly."

"That's most certainly right, and you did well nevertheless."

Tuss was startled by the sound. He looked about. Eyes bright and curious. Then he remembered the booming voice that'd surprised him and sent him on his unplanned trip into the brush.

"Correction young one. You did better than well. I can honestly say that I've seldom, if ever, seen an experienced adult fly as skillfully as you just did."

"Oh!" he exclaimed when he realized that the huge dragonfly was right in front of him. It was the first that he'd seen up close. The giant male had to be at least three times Tuss' size.

His mind flashed back to when the Teachers and Elders were no more than blurry, unclear outlines perched in the open air just above the Fen's rippling surface. This was totally different however; there was nothing between him and this huge living form. Tuss felt very vulnerable, completely exposed, and wondered if something bad was about to happen.

When enough time had passed and nothing awful came about, he looked the stranger over.

Before him hovered a dragonfly that was brown from back to front with brilliant green and blue rings running along his entire length. His eyes were large and complex. They whirled in shades of the same browns, greens and blues that marked his body. Tuss was mesmerized. He'd never seen the eyes of his own kind before, at least not above the murky waters of his old home.

"Well? Did you knock yourself speechless? Or are you just being rude?" asked the huge flier.

Tuss needed to think a bit before answering. He had no point of reference, was he in trouble? Was this massive dragonfly mad at him? He'd no idea what to expect and therefore had no idea what to say. He knew a confrontation could only end badly for him.

"Well?" This time a deep rumble accompanied the question.

"Ummm, sorry. I'm not speechless. I'm just a little, uh, surprised is all," Tuss finally answered wondering if he was actually hearing laughter.

"Okay, that's better. I was afraid for a moment that you were just another rude dragonfly, newly emerged, too young and foolish to respond to a reasonable question."

"No sir. I'm newly emerged but I'm pretty sure that I'm not rude. At least, if I was just now, I didn't mean to be."

"Good enough. But, don't call me sir. I'm called Aurantium, but you my new young friend may call me Auran. There's no sense using proper names and such amongst friends. They're very tedious to pronounce and a little too formal in my humble opinion."

Tuss heard the rumbling sound coming from the huge dragonfly again and realized that, yes, it was laughter he'd heard before.

"Well then, I'm glad to make your acquaintance Auran, sir…" Tuss began.

"Now what did I just say? It's Auran, just Auran, no *sir* attached, please and thank you very much. As I said, there's no need for such formalities with me."

"Okay, I'll do my best to remember, Auran. I'm Tussilago, everyone calls me Tuss."

"Tuss, is it?"

"Yes sir, uhm I mean, yes Auran."

"Ah yes, good then. Tuss, that's what I'll call you then. We can henceforth dispense with the formal names and titles. They're unnecessarily pretentious, don't you think?"

Tuss agreed with the huge dragonfly knowing that his opinion wasn't really needed, "I sure do."

"We're just two friendly dragonflies, happy to make each other's acquaintance."

Tuss' mind filled with a thousand questions and conflicting thoughts. His nervousness took control of his mouth and he blurted, "so much about our ways, our Tradition, the whole independence thing. I thought for a moment there, we were going to battle right here. I crossed into your territory." He took a deep breath and tried to slow down. "That's what you were just talking about right? When you said

28

something about *'formalities and how all of it seems a bit pretentious'*." He couldn't stop himself, though he desperately wanted to. He'd just met this friendly fellow and didn't want to offend; but still he went on, "and my friends feel the same way as I do and..."

"Hold on there, Tuss," Auran paused, looked around cautiously before he went on, "you'll need to be very careful about speaking so boldly." He paused again, this time he looked more reflective than cautious. When he spoke his voice sounded sad and distant. "It's not like you're going to be saying much of anything to anyone, boldly, out loud or otherwise."

"That's what I was afraid of. It's because of the whole Tradition thing, right?" Tuss asked.

"I have to answer with a yes and a no."

"I'm not sure I understand," Tuss couldn't keep the confusion out of his voice. He was beginning to like this strange dragonfly. By the look of him he'd been through quite a lot over the span of his life. There were scars all along his sides and minor tatters and tears on all four of his wings.

"I'm sorry for being so vague, Tuss, so let me restate it as plainly as possible. You've been taught that dragonflies live by a Tradition, one that's suited perfectly to our nature. As you know, it's why we live out our lives in isolation and more popularly described, our independence."

"Yeah, I understand that much. It seemed like it was all that we were taught. None of us liked the idea of living alone, not for the rest of our lives. It doesn't sound like such a great thing, but you answered me with a yes and a no."

"I did. You listen well, I better keep that in mind." Auran laughed quietly to himself again before continuing. "The answer is firstly yes because our Tradition is all about following our natural tendencies which in turn helps keep things peaceful amongst our kind. And I guess

I answered no because deep down inside I feel that we should rise above all of that and deny the more negative aspects of our nature, Tradition or no Tradition."

"You're saying that we should ignore our Tradition?"

"No. Not in so many words and," Auran looked all about, once again making sure that no one was near enough to hear what he was about to say, "it's the cornerstone of our lives, our law. Maybe, it's all that keeps us civil; but I'll never understand why we don't seek ways to honor it even as we seek to live, how do I best state this, less legalistic and isolated lives."

"Oh!" Tuss looked more closely at his new acquaintance, hoping he'd heard right. He couldn't keep the excitement from his voice, the idea that he and his friends wouldn't have to separate from one another for good, was too much, "are you saying that..."

Auran cut him off with a long, sad sigh. "Slow down Tuss, relax and hear me out. I'm saying that we do live by the Tradition as you've been taught but I'm also saying that I can see the possibility for eventual, advised changes, if you will." He sighed again, and added almost as if only to himself, "it's all such a shame, what we've become."

Tuss felt his excitement begin to deflate. "So all of that stuff we were taught really is true? My friends and I will have to keep ourselves separate?"

"I'm afraid so. It's our way, we're dragonflies after all." A touch of bitterness filled Auran's last words.

It can't be! I can't spend the rest of my life alone! I just can't! The very thought of it all hurt Tuss deeply. He'd always imagined or hoped that the teachings were more like living guidelines, and real life counsel, not absolute regulations that must be adhered to, unquestionably.

"But, ummm," Tuss hardly knew what he wanted to say so he stopped. He couldn't believe that in just one day his life was changing so drastically.

"But?" Auran asked him.

"But what about my friends, Auran? I can't forget that they exist. The time we spent together before meant something, it had to. I can't let that go." Anger began to course through him, "I won't!" Tuss didn't know how his huge new friend would respond to such a forceful statement from a recently emerged youngster. He waited for a response; it came in the form of the same deep, rumbling laughter.

"You're laughing? It's not funny Auran, it's horrible actually." His anger grew hotter.

"Easy now young Tuss, there's no need to be angry with me. I was laughing true, but not at you. What you said fills me with joy, so I laugh."

Tuss was so stunned he'd forgotten exactly what he'd just said. "Huh, me?"

"You have a fire inside of you. I respect that and even more so, because you're correct. And I'll tell you something else. You aren't the first young dragonfly that I've spoken with today that's said the very same thing in almost the very same words."

"Really? Who?"

"I'm not at liberty to reveal that right now. Don't look so disappointed. My guess is that you'll find out on your own before too long," Auran could see that Tuss was still bothered, "and I'm sorry that my laughter offended you, it wasn't intended for ill. I was laughing at the coincidence."

"What coincidence? I'm confused again."

"Let me explain. In all my life, and all my interactions with the newly emerged, in one day I meet two that are so much alike and yet so different from all that have come before," Auran paused for a bit until he realized that Tuss was waiting for him to finish, "I shouldn't say more, not yet anyway. I hope that's good enough?"

"I guess it has to be." Tuss wasn't completely satisfied but Auran had said that he would learn more and soon.

After a short silence, Tuss felt the need to clear his conscience, "I'm sorry for my outburst about Tradition, Auran. I know I shouldn't be angry but it sure feels right to be mad at the way things are. What you said, even though I already knew it was true, it seems so unfair."

"Tussilago, I don't blame you for being upset and I certainly don't hold your passion against you. Many aspects of life seem unfair when you're young, and I suppose that some truly are.

It gets harder to make those distinctions as you age. You'll find that out for yourself one day. But, you'll also find that I'm not like most of the others. For instance, if you hadn't realized yet, I'm not an advocate of the current way in which we honor our Tradition."

Tuss looked around on impulse, whatever paranoia Auran had displayed about being overheard, was catchy.

Auran hovered closer to him and spoke in a conspiratorial tone. "Of course, my friend, you can never tell anyone what I just said. There are pretenses we elderly fliers must sometimes keep."

"I won't," Tuss said, mirroring the tone. "You keep calling me your friend? Are we allowed to be friends?"

Auran's laughter rumbled out louder than ever. "Who's to stop us? The Tradition grants us our independence doesn't it? The other young dragonfly I spoke with today asked that very same question, too. But never mind about that particular individual for now. As I said, it's not for me to speak any more about that conversation, it's a matter of propriety and such, you must understand."

"Yeah, I guess." Tuss realized that all of his anger was gone; replacing it was a new sense of peace. The idea of having friends had always been an important part of his pre-emerged life and on his first day of freedom, he'd made a new one. "Friends," he muttered aloud without realizing it.

"Yes, friends, and as far as I am concerned, we've been since the moment we met. I hope you feel the same. It would mean a lot to me. There's something different, something special about you and..." Auran left that thought unfinished too. Tuss realized that Auran had a habit of doing that.

"I do feel that way and I'm glad we met, but I don't know anything about being special." Tuss looked off into the distance, his mind was filled with too much new information, "I just didn't expect to meet someone so soon and especially not one that was so old."

Once again, the deep laughter filled the air.

"Oops! Sorry," Tuss apologized.

"Nonsense! No need to apologize for simply stating the obvious when amongst friends." Auran's kind words assured Tuss that all was well.

They hovered together for a time in companionable silence, enjoying each other's company.

Auran interrupted the quiet, "I don't know if you've noticed or not Tuss but the day is starting to move along towards evening."

"Oh no! I didn't," Tuss was overwhelmed with dread; he didn't really know what to do when night fell. No one had told him about that part of post-emergence life. *Or*, he thought, *if they did, I must not have been paying attention*. Which was all too likely.

"Don't look so worried, there's still enough evening remaining for you to explore a bit more. The Fen is big; you won't have any trouble finding a spot to spend the night. Try and forget about the negatives we spoke of, focus on the here and now. This is your first day as a creature of the air, go test out your wings and enjoy your new life as a dragonfly, but remember, don't fly too high!"

"Yeah, I almost learned that one the worst possible way."

"Humph! You're here, talking with me, so that means," Auran saw

The DragonTree

Tuss shudder, "it was a bird?"

"Yes, a big one. It missed me and then seemed to forget about me. I don't know why it left me alone after the first pass but it was too close. I don't really want to dwell on it."

"Ah! Learn from the experience Tussilago, birds are dangerous, always hungry and thankfully very forgetful. Be sure to keep a constant vigil, check the skies when you're in the open and always, always pay attention to where you are at all times."

"Thank you sir, I mean Auran, I will, but," he paused, embarrassed to ask, "ummm, where do I stay the night? You said the Fen is big but I don't know where to begin, I know our kind don't fly well when it's cool. I'm a bit worried, no one has told me where to go or what to do."

"See now, that's part of the Tradition, foolish as it may seem. You're supposed to find an area you like, one that's unoccupied or, if you're willing to contend, one that's occupied."

"Contend?" Tuss asked, unable to keep the concern out of his voice.

Auran looked at the surprised Tuss and laughed. "That, my young friend, will not be necessary. As I said the Fen is large and there are plenty of open spaces along its shore. I suggest that you look to the north where the swamp flows in through the large reed fields. No one is likely to bother you up there."

"Bother me?" Tuss asked.

"Never mind about that now. In time, it'll all make sense," Auran answered. "Now I must bid you a good day. Before you leave, though, I want you to know that you're always welcome to come here. Forget all that you've heard about territory and challenges when you think of this area and your new friend, Auran. Come and visit with me anytime."

"Thank you, I will. I'll want someone to talk to. The idea of independence and isolation is so depressing. I'm already feeling sad and lonely."

"Don't let that trouble your thoughts tonight, Tussilago. You have tomorrow ahead of you with all its wonders. It'll be a new day, filled with possibilities and endless discoveries. Go on now, but don't forget about this old flier. When all that's new makes you forgetful and tries to take you up and carry you away, remember, I'm always here."

"I won't forget. Farewell Auran and thanks!" Tuss forced himself to turn away. He paused a moment, wanting to ask one more question that seemed important, "Auran, how big is the Fen? You said it's large and that there's plenty of space but it seems like I can fly across it in no time."

"Ah yes, good question. Distance is a funny thing for dragonflies."

"Funny how?" Tuss was genuinely curious.

"Take our personal spaces, those we're supposed to patrol. I can traverse mine hundreds of times a day. Please don't tell anyone, but I occasionally overlap my neighbors, just not when they're looking." Auran laughed at his joke. "Ignore the poor attempt at humor. We can travel very great distances very quickly when we need or want, but we patrol slowly. Remember what I said about vigilance? Slow is careful." He gave Tuss a stern look hoping to drive the point home. "So, while the Fen may seem small when we fly at top speed, for our daily lives and routines, it's considerably larger in surface area than our folk have ever needed. There's room for many times our current population."

"Okay! That makes sense, speed shortens distances. At least it gives that impression. Travel under water was so slow!" The concepts of size, space and emptiness saddened Tuss all over again, *it's so big, so empty and yet I can fly across it in no time, but why would I need to if I'm to live in constant isolation?*

Fighting both sorrow and loneliness he flew towards the north shore. Before he went far he heard Auran's voice once more, "goodbye for now, young Tussilago."

After flying for a distance, Tuss turned about and looked back to where his new friend lived. His negative emotions were swept away in the rising admiration that filled his heart and mind. He was seeing the towering DragonTree in its fullness for only the second time in his young, airborne life.

"How could I have missed it from below? I was crawling in its shadow so many times." Tuss wasn't even aware that he was speaking again. A Giant Skimmer passing close by gave him a hard stare before moving on.

He hovered there for a long instance, regarding the landmark, central to the histories and tales of his kind. He was looking at the Tree that was the namesake for his folk and for his home.

Tuss was seeing the DragonTree, really seeing it for the first time. The earlier occasion seemed like a dream to him now, this was reality at a whole new level, and it was incredible.

A breeze was blowing, slight but enough to create unwanted aerodynamic lift to his wings. A blood freezing shriek came to him from the west, beyond the great Tree. *Is that a bird?* He realized that he was rising further above the water.

"I've had enough excitement today. And that especially applies to the sort of danger involving predatory beasts that think I'm food!" He dipped his head and shot across the Fen angling northward, swiping at the small flying insects that were his own source of food. "Now I'm the predator!" He laughed as he went.

Chapter Four

Other Watchers

Auran's eyes weren't the only ones that watched Tuss speed away.

***

Something has changed and it's not good...

Another group of Hive's spies had found the Fen. They were coming in from the west just as the others were departing to the east. The proximity allowed the sub-queens to link together; the group-mind was strong, the distance was not so great. Their communication was sharp and concise, one group led by Second would fly to Hive and report, the other led by Third would stay behind and continue to gather information. The more the Queen knew about these silly creatures the better. The Imperative was clear on the issue; Hive could not share any region with any creature that might be a threat. The dragonflies preferred the wetland regions but traveled far enough abroad to merit attention.

What the newest arrivals saw was distressing. Some of the strange creatures had communed together and by all visible accounts had shared thoughts and words. For the Queen of Hive, this kind of behavior was a mockery, only minions of Hive could be tolerated to share intelligence or a common mind. The Imperative pulsed through the watchers.

They must die for this...We are Legion...We are Hive...We shall conquer...

Their mutual hate and anger were powerful. It emanated from the group-mind like an unseen vapor. It pulsed from them in a wave that spread in all directions, invisible, affecting every sentient creature it touched with its passing.

***

A Kingbird on the verge of capturing the day's meal, one that would feed her young, missed her prey as the dread touch of the malignant mind grazed her senses. Her small family would endure the night, hungry.

A young mouse crawled from hiding and out into a clearing in the western meadow. It'd been taught well by its father and had never made such a deadly mistake before. Its mind was clouded with fear and greatly confused by something it couldn't identify. A Coopers Hawk perched at the edge of the west wood, waiting for some unsuspecting quarry, swooped down upon the unwary mouse. The powerful raptor, with the struggling mouse clutched in its talons was beginning its ascent when it shuddered violently. It wasn't immune to the effect of the unseen terror. Its talons opened reflexively, the young mouse dropped into the thick grass at the edge of the meadow. Having lost it's prey the hawk shrieked a fearsome call, one meant to warn whatever it was that had interrupted its hunting.

The mouse, undamaged by the talons but shaken and hurting from the fall, scurried back into cover and shivered with fright.

The ever noisy crickets ceased their stridulation; birds stopped chirping and the croaking of the frogs quieted. The sense of danger felt by all living creatures increased, the entire region fell silent.

All of the sounds of the DragonTree Fen, the buzzing, humming, splashing, whooshing and whirring quit. There was a breathless pause, one in which the hustle and bustle of life's activity ceased. A hush filled the world, even the breeze seemed to still.

***

Second and Third broke their malevolent commune. The bees, under the command of Third, turned as one and faded into the shadows of the forest. Second continued eastward.

***

Noises and stirrings began to fill the world once again as the sense of danger faded. Peace had returned. The hearts of the creatures that lived in and about the Fen beat slower.

There was one exception.

Speyeria-Idalia, a bright orange butterfly spotted with black, white and brown, usually spent her days in the east meadows. Earlier, she'd decided to fly to the west. It was a long way around the shores of the Fen but she loved the solitude she usually found there. Today however, was different, after what she'd seen and felt. *Well, I must reconsider never coming back, even though the flowers here are so lovely...* Lovely or not, she wasn't sure that she'd ever feel safe again in this remote spot. The little meadow had always been perfect for quiet meditation. She could browse the flowers after the manner of her kind and make her observations. That's what butterflies did after all and this was a great place for both activities, since typically there were so few distractions. Her mind was confused. The terror she'd felt was fading away, but she doubted that she could ever forget the look of the malevolent bees. Her internal struggles were concluded when she realized that she liked this quiet place more than she feared them. She needed to spend more time considering. Events weren't always what they seemed at first and what they might mean tomorrow could be different from today.

She would speak to her friend Speyeria-Nokomis. His advice would be invaluable; he was the one other butterfly that seemed to understand her. He knew how very different she was from the rest of their community. He was the only one that she could talk with when things in the greater world bothered her. And like her, he wasn't like the others, not closed off to new ideas. He even listened when she mentioned her concerns about the needs and welfare of other creatures.

"One more day of thought will I give it, so to say. Then and not after, I'll no longer come to this place, if peace I cannot find." Idalia spoke out loud, knowing that she was alone and that none would hear her. She was one of the few of her kind that liked to use her voice, strange as it was. All butterflies could speak, but they seldom did. One of the funny things about them, one reason they didn't speak often was that when they did, their words came out in a confusing fashion. They could think as clearly as the next creature but when they tried to translate thought into words it came out jumbled and strange.

Our speech flutters all about, much like we do when we fly, but one day, she thought, *I'll speak as clearly as I can think, but that requires practice and none of my kind is willing to do so with me, none beside Nokomis.*

With her considerations completed, Idalia decided to take another risk, something else her kind rarely did. She would tempt fate and short cut her way across the open water of the DragonTree Fen. It made her feel more alive because doing so was different and exciting.

As she flew, she looked down at the water knowing that simply brushing the surface with a single wingtip would be the end of her. She wasn't afraid though, she'd flown this way before. The simple pleasure of looking down and seeing her orange beauty reflected below was attraction enough. Add the fact that none of the others would do what she was doing, *well, I like that I'm not as Creed-bound as they.*

The evening began to fade as she fluttered towards the safety of the eastern meadows. Once there, she would once more feel the comfort of the well known world and of course have time to ponder all she'd seen and heard.

***

For the first time in many generations of DragonTree, life was about to change. None of the residents besides an observant but slightly confused butterfly had the slimmest clue about what was coming.

They would find out soon enough, though.

Chapter Five

A Friendship Renewed

The very next day, Tuss bumped into, literally, he bumped into one of his friends.

The lesson from the day before, *'pay attention to where you're going'* was completely forgotten. He hadn't slept well, there were too many new things that occupied his thoughts. His mind had raced around in circles all night. So instead of paying attention to where he was going, he allowed himself to daydream just as he had before meeting Auran. It was a bad habit. *Only two days of life in the air and I'm falling into the same old routines. Then again, what had happened, turned out to be the best part of my day.*

"Hey, watch it!"

He was startled from his thoughts by the pleasant voice even as he bumped headlong into the side of its owner. He'd just time enough to think, *not this again,* before he corrected himself and looked at his most recent victim. She was a blue dragonfly with brown and yellow striations, but not just a blue dragonfly; she was a Blue Dasher just like he was.

"Do you ever watch where you're going?"

He couldn't hide his surprise at the question, "do I ever? Huh?"

"Yeah! Do you ever pay attention to where you're going?"

"I uhhh, are you okay? I didn't hurt you did I?"

"I'm fine thanks but really now, two days in a row?" She began to laugh, which was pleasant enough, but Tuss felt himself coloring with embarrassment anyway.

"I'm sorry," he muttered.

"Don't be, I said I'm fine. You don't listen either?" Her tone was teasing but Tuss didn't sense any meanness. "Same old Tuss..." She let her voice trail off into that pleasant sounding laughter once more.

A strange feeling overcame him then, he knew that voice. He'd only talked to one actual dragonfly before now but even so, *I know that I know this female.* He looked her over more carefully. She was most definitely a female Blue Dasher, but not as large as he was. She was more brown than blue along her abdomen and there were yellow stripes running down her entire length. Only her long segmented tale section had portions that were the same color blue as his.

"Well?" she asked after putting up with his inspection for long enough.

He managed to stammer out, "sorry, yeah I do watch where I'm going. Or I usually did or I do I mean but..."

She laughed again. He liked the sound even more the second time, it was sweet just like her voice. As she continued to laugh, his feeling of familiarity grew. *Something about that laugh.*

"Go on," she reminded, "you were saying something about how you watch out?"

"I do, but I'm new to this whole flying thing. There's so much to take in and I keep getting distracted. It's an old habit I've not been able to shake," he admitted.

"Yeah it's new to me too but I haven't flown around dreaming and crashing into others like you have. Truth be told though, I almost flew straight into the Tree early yesterday morning."

"Hey! Me too. Yesterday though," he stopped realizing the she didn't

44

say *a tree* but *The Tree.* "You mean the DragonTree, right?"

"That's the one, it's something else, isn't it?"

"It sure is, but," Tuss stopped speaking and looked at her again. *Why does she keep implying that she knows something about how my day went?* It bothered him, made him a little mad even. He finally asked, "do I know you? Have we met before?"

When she laughed again, he knew. His heart filled with joy and excitement. "Cas? It's really you?"

"Yeah it's me, Tuss. Wings and all!"

He looked more closely, amazed at the changes. Just a couple days ago she'd been a little brown water-dragon, not unattractive but nothing like she was now. As a dragonfly Cas was beautiful beyond description. Her form was long and sleek, she had that fearsome shape much like his own, *we're so much alike!*

"Are you going to say something or just hover there and gawk at me?" Her tone was teasing just as he remembered. Was it only a day or so ago? Before him was his dearest friend, raised from the depths of the Fen, transformed into something more stunning than he could've imagined.

"Yeah, uhmmm no, sorry!" He stopped stammering long enough to take a deep breath and start over. "Hi, Cas. I can't believe it's actually you. I just never expected, I mean, wow! It's really you. What a great surprise!"

"Thanks! I'm happy to see you too." Her colors glowed in the bright sunlight, proof beyond words that her joy at the accidental meeting was equal to his. "Can you believe that we're both Blue Dashers? What're the odds?"

"I can't. I never even considered the likelihood before but it's pretty cool now that we know." He considered, "It's sort of odd that we never talked about what types of dragonflies we'd be. We talked about everything else."

45

"Yeah. I guess it was enough just knowing that we were going to be dragonflies. But Tuss, have you seen the others yet? They're all so different."

"All different?" He asked, "You've seen some of the others? I only actually met one dragonfly yesterday. I saw lots of others but not up close. I must've emerged more slowly than you did."

"Not just some of them Tuss, all of them, all seven."

"Really? How were you able to find them? The Fen's so huge."

"It's not that big and anyhow, it wasn't that hard. I just flew around looking for young dragonflies that seemed lost and distracted. You know, just like you were right before you flew into me."

"Oh! That makes sense. I wish I'd thought of it."

"You probably would've, eventually."

"Yeah right! I'm too busy daydreaming and bumping into things. Oh yeah, and I had a pretty close call with a bird too."

"You what? How close?" Cas was incredulous.

"Let's say that I was one wing-stroke away from not meeting you or anyone else for that matter, ever." He shuddered with the memory.

"TUSS!" All the reprimand Cas would ever need to level at him existed in just his name.

"I know Cas, I know! Auran, the dragonfly I met yesterday, let me have it too. You can probably guess why it happened, I was thinking; well, you know."

"Daydreaming as always. Same old Tuss."

"Yeah that's me. But let's forget that for now and back up a bit. How again did you find the others when I couldn't?"

"Well, it was easier for me. I emerged closer to them than you did. I couldn't see you once we climbed out of the water, but I could see some of them."

"You did? Who?"

"Coria and I actually shared the same reed; Aneth and Leon were just a couple over from us. We could hear Briza complaining the entire time. Of all the things to transform first, it had to be his mouth."

"Ha! That's not surprising."

"I found Ace, Mira and Gal soon after I was able to fly. They were together and looking for the rest of us. They must've emerged and changed faster than we did. I guess that means you were the last and we unintentionally left you behind while searching for each other. Sorry about that. But it explains why we didn't find you."

"Well that figures. I spent all of yesterday alone except for when I was speaking to my new friend." He sighed with relief knowing now that today would be different. "You know, waiting for the changes to finish, drying in the sunlight, it seemed like it would take forever. And then when it was done, I was so happy to be rid of that underwater shell and able to fly, time seemed to speed up. Was it the same for you, Cas?"

"Sort of, but Coria was near me and we were able to talk as we waited. Being near a friend made the time pass quickly." She paused thinking about what he'd just said. "You mentioned a new friend. That would be the dragonfly you almost bumped into, like you did with me?"

"How could you know that?" Tuss thought back to the day before and remembered Auran saying something about a meeting he wasn't willing to talk about. "You met Auran too? It was you he was refusing to talk about?"

"Yes and yes. Yesterday, just after the others and I decided to go our separate ways. All of us wanted to explore the Fen. So I flew straight to the Tree. I wanted to see it up close, we'd been told so much about it. It's so beautiful."

"It sure is, and I guess that's when you met him. He patrols that entire area."

Cass and Tuss

"Yeah and I saw him again this morning, he's so nice. Hey! Remember how we used to play games of Capture in and around all those strange tree roots?"

"You mean the Tangle? The ones that form the really cool maze and then plunge way down into the deep water?" he asked.

"That's it, I actually forgot the name. They're the roots of the DragonTree you know. They grow out from it, down the bank and deep into the Fen. Can you believe that all those times we were playing, lost in the fun, we never knew what the DragonTree was really like? Think about it Tuss, all the stories about it and yet we didn't realize."

"Yeah, but how could we?" His thoughts drifted back, remembering how much time they'd spent there. It was by far their favorite place to gather at least until near the end of their life underwater.

***

Tuss was sick of being a nymph and living through what he assumed would be the most excruciating time of his life. The days of one boring class followed by another boring class, the feeling of being trapped in an unforgiving, underwater world. All of it was finally nearing an end. Knowing the time of emergence was close made the waiting worse. Time was crawling too slowly for him. He'd seen far too many days that were little different one from another. He was tired of the constant threat posed by predators, from the shores, from the deep and even the environment itself. He hated how the dangers restricted nymphs to the *safer* but too confined regions in the shallows. It was only minimally safer anyway, a matter of degrees safer, but still *safe* if-they-stayed-away-from-the-swampy-regions-in-the-north-where-the-frogs-though-slow-and-stupid-as-could-be-were-ready-to-eat-anyone-careless-enough-to-wander-out-of-cover-safe. Or *safe* if they stayed away from the south where the Fen emptied itself through a narrow opening in the rocky shelves that rose up from the black depths. There, deadly currents swept away any foolish creature; be they fish, insect or amphibian into the unknown. It was where an invisible, inescapable vortex, dragged anyone unfortunate enough to venture too close to a horrible fate. And *safe* if they didn't attract the attention of the mindless but ever-hungry fish. Some of which were so big, Tuss wondered why they even bothered wasting time trying to eat his kind. But they did, and the frogs did and the currents did, so much else did too, and it all added up to the fact that death seemed to be present everywhere, even when they played their *unsanctioned* games.

He remembered the Tangle and breaking into teams to play a version of *Hold-the-high-ground.* A game where one team would try and fend off another any way they were able. Things could get rough to a point just shy of serious injury. They were water-dragons; the nymphs of dragonflies in waiting, in a single word, deadly. Tuss was never truly comfortable with what some of the games did to them. He liked his friends, he liked the peace and camaraderie that could exist between them and would hate to see any of them hurt. But the way they played in the Tangle changed something in all of them. He wasn't so sure the changes were constructive. Either way, gaming or just living was a challenge for everyone. And there was always the possibility that one of them would be lost for good, it had happened to others. They were after all, small creatures in a large dangerous world. All of them knew of hatch-mates that'd disappeared and typically with no one there to witness and never any way to know what actually happened. And so they played, heedless of the risk and ignored who and what they became, it was their only means of escape from the ordinary.

Aneth however was different from the others. He was the largest and strongest of the friends. He could physically dominate any of them any time he desired. His essential character didn't change when at play. Instead, he chose to act like they were all physical equals. That was just one example of what his friends did with and for each other. It created the unity they shared and had come to love and rely upon.

It was Aneth and Gal that together kept all of them in check, Aneth because he was gentle and Gal because he was logical. None dared argue with the two of them, particularly if they agreed about something pertaining to the games.

And here they were, ready to begin what would be their last underwater engagements. They had chosen the Tangle.

Briza, Coria, Leon, Aneth, Acer, Mira and a few nymphs Tuss wasn't too familiar with, would hold the high ground first. Gal, Cas and Tuss were joined for the first time by Ophrys, Heleni and a couple of their hatching group. The teams had even numbers, which was unusual. Tuss' close friends numbered nine and had only just recently started to include others. They hadn't been intentionally exclusive before but their classmates hadn't shown any open interest in the *silly* activities. It was the Teachers that referred to the games as silly. According to them, the nymphs were supposed to spend their free time alone. It was supposedly good practice for their mature life, above the surface. It was Ophrys that first approached them and asked if they could join in. Briza's immediate response was 'definitely not'; Coria's was 'absolutely'. The argument raged for days and led to Briza's eventual snubbing of Coria. And since the nine of them usually hung together as a group, his stubbornness forced him to snub the rest of them by association. Briza had tried to form friendships and bonds with other nymphs but nothing ever came close to what the original nine enjoyed.

Then one day, none of them had actually kept track of how many, he was just there, back among them again. Briza of old, brash, outspoken and troublesome, acting as if nothing had ever happened. The friction and argument between he and Coria, was just a *silly misunderstanding.* In his absence he'd somehow fully formed in his mind the concept that the original group was a "League". When asked to explain he told them, "we're friends to the end, a team, in league, for whatever!" He said that they needed to remain "inseparable, a league of comrades, ready to face all comers."

So there they were in the Tangle, together playing the last game of their lives.

"Now!" Gal shouted. Underwater shouts were just stronger versions of the vibrations created when they talked. They'd been taught that their voices, once they emerged, would have levels of expression and tonality, which in their present state, they couldn't begin to imagine.

Cas and Tuss moved together up the south rise of the Tangle where small gaps in the roots allowed them to keep in tight cover that offered overhead protection. Aneth and Leon being larger, couldn't reach them and drive them back, the others were too small to pull them out. Approaching the objective this way, the two only had to fend off attacks from the front. They progressed one after the other in short darting spurts that used energy sparingly and drove Coria, Ace and Mira steadily backwards and upwards. Briza was angrily awaiting his chance to get involved but was thus far unsuccessful. The three females were determined to stop Cas and Tuss from advancing and refused to give up their positions to him. Ophrys and Heleni led the other attackers from the north and more open ground. They were much larger, able to keep Leon and Aneth busy. None could attack from the east or west. The Tangle was in a narrow gap between the shoreline and the watery deeps. It was this confined setting that made it so much fun to play this particular game in this particular location.

It was also this setting that allowed for the unthinkable to happen.

Briza, enraged at being left out of the action, abandoned the south side of the defense and crawled his way over the high ground to see if he could help Aneth and Leon. They were hard pressed by the slightly smaller, more numerous and speedier attackers. Aneth saw Briza, called for him to move to the eastern edge of the Tangle where it dropped off steeply into the deep and hold there. He did as asked, ready for action. He could see that Ophrys, followed closely by Heleni, was about to crest the rise. He charged, ready to take both on at once, not caring that they had him two-to-one and that both were much larger.

They began to shout out their battle cries, certain that victory was theirs, when a speeding shadow loomed up from the murky depths. It approached from behind with maw gaping wide. They had no chance to react. Briza had no time to warn them, even if he had, there was nothing they could've done. The fish had them in a quick flashing strike. It missed Briza by the slimmest margin as it rushed by just over him. The forward wash of the monster's large body passing so closely pulled him lose from his precarious purchase and swept him out and over the depths. He was clearly in shock, doing nothing to arrest his fall, about to drop into the abyss when Aneth moving faster than Tuss believed possible, reached out a desperate tarsi and was just able to grab Briza's shell. Off balance and overextended, he began to lose his grip on the slippery root. He was about to follow the sinking Briza down when Leon and Mira working together anchored themselves, formed a chain, linked tarsi to tarsi and caught Aneth's shell. The rest of them, at first frozen in place by horror and disbelief, finally shook themselves into action and rushed to their aid.

Once safe, they huddled together for a time trying to come to grips with what had just happened. All of the warnings, the threats and admonitions to be careful were now, all too real for the survivors. They'd just experienced a life changing event, one they would never be able to forget.

Briza was the first to break the silence, "that's proof that I've been right all along."

"Briza!" Cas was angry. "You can't be making a joke at a time like this?"

"What if I am?" He replied back just as angrily.

"Hey now, stop it! You two, please don't. Now's not the time." Tuss didn't want emotions to spiral out of control; he knew that everyone was feeling brittle enough as is.

"But Tuss, he..."

"He nothing Cas, it's me Briza and yeah I do joke and act the fool often enough. Too often for your tastes I'm sure, but not this time. I was just thinking out loud I guess, saying what I should've kept to myself. But I didn't and I won't apologize. No matter how mad you get. I'll say this though. What I was thinking about, in full, was; I've been right all along, we are a league of friends. If we weren't I'd be dead too.

They looked at him.

"You didn't let me fall," he said to Aneth, Leon and Mira. All of them could see the fear return to his eyes, he looked diminished. He wasn't the Briza they were used to, he wasn't joking or teasing.

"No," Aneth said. "We didn't let you fall."

Cas, seeing Briza's humbled state, relaxed just enough for them to talk things out. Acer and Mira wanted to report the loss of their nymph friends to some authority but were reminded by Gal that there wasn't an *authority* that would care, or even if they did care, were powerless to do anything about it. He reminded them that they were on their own; supposedly practicing their individuality, learning how proper dragonflies behaved, indifferent to any other but themselves. Therefore the loss of their contemporaries shouldn't matter.

Gal silently began to take a head count. He reported later, when the rest were more able to deal with the terrible news that three of the others, those that had come with Ophrys were missing too. There was a search a day later but they were never found and presumed to be lost as well. Gal could be like that, coldly logical but reserved when the needs of others demanded.

"I know that's all true but it's horrible. No one cares, there's no community, no compassion, nothing but disinterest. I hate how our kind chooses to live up above!" Tuss complained.

"They say it's our way, the best means for self-preservation," Gal stated objectively. "The histories teach that if we didn't hold to the absolute formality of Tradition we'd destroy one another and eventually our entire kind."

"Yeah they say that, but you see the flaw in that right?" Briza asked.

"I do Briza," Gal agreed. "The violent competition over space along the Fen's shore only perpetuates more violence. Solitude fosters ignorance of others and their needs, wants or desires."

"It's why I went along with Tuss when he first asked me to rebel against Tradition by following Tradition, but in a different way," Cas added in that voice that Tuss loved to hear. Her vocal vibrations were like none other's.

*****

"Tuss, TUSS!"

He pulled his mind back to the present, startled by the overlapping sound of Cas' voice from memory with that of the here and now. He shook himself to clear his head. "Oops! Sorry Cas."

"Daydreaming? In the middle of our first conversation? And when we were talking about the problem you have with daydreaming no less, Tuss!" She sounded exasperated.

"Yeah, I was just remembering that last day in the Tangle."

"Oh! That was a bad time. I'm glad we'll never have to go back under to those old places, not while we live at least."

They both paused and reflected, the gloomy memories clouding their minds on this bright day. It didn't last long; Cas wasn't the type to dwell on the past. She picked up where they'd left off, "Well, we finally know now what was above us back then. And think about it. We can do more than scramble about the roots; we can fly circles around it anytime we want. Auran told me that I was welcome to visit him whenever I like."

"Me, too. He's really great. I spoke to him again this morning, that's how I knew you met him, he even told me what you looked like."

"And?" Tuss asked.

"And what?" Cas replied.

"And what do you think? How do I look?"

"You look better than I would've expected, almost presentable."

"Hah! You'd better be careful. We're both Blue Dashers. An insult to me is an insult to you."

"I didn't insult you. I'm just not willing to stroke your ego is all. But don't worry, you look really good Tuss...a bit scary, but in a good way."

"What about the others, Cas? Are any Blue Dashers too?"

"Oh no, none of them are. In fact, of the nine of us, you and I are the only two that are alike."

"Really? That's strange isn't it?"

"Sort of, but not totally strange. Don't forget how many types of dragonflies live here at the Fen."

"I haven't forgotten but I've only met Auran and you so far. And you can't possibly think that I'd forgotten those endlessly boring lessons about history and kinds and types? You know it's funny though?"

"What is?"

"All of those lessons about what we are and about the Tradition, when what I really wanted to hear was the old stories and legends, you know, the interesting stuff, about this very Tree." He looked at it as he finished speaking.

"Uh-huh, you and Briza both. And speaking of him, he's going to be incorrigible now."

"Why? Is there something wrong with him?"

"No, but I almost wish there was. The problem, he's too handsome. He's a Banded Pennant, all dark blue and sleek, with black striped wings. He looks fearsome and lovely at the same time. I bet he'll spend most of his days simply looking at his reflection in the water."

"Great! That's all we needed. Still, I can't wait to see him. What about the others?"

"I'll tell you what. If you can be patient for one more day, you'll see them for yourself."

"Oh?" Tuss was instantly curious.

She moved closer and spoke quietly, her voice sly, "we've planned a meeting for tomorrow."

"You have? Already?" Tuss couldn't hide his surprise.

Cas noticed it and was worried that he was bothered because he hadn't been part of the planning. "Yeah Tuss, we couldn't find you. We made the plans without your input. You're not mad are you?"

"Mad, me?"

"Yeah, you. It wouldn't be the first time. Well?"

"No Cas, I'm not mad. But I'm a little worried. I thought having a meeting wouldn't be allowed, you know, with the Tradition and all?"

"I asked Auran about that and his answer was a bit odd, very unclear. I got the impression that he didn't want to either encourage or discourage us. I ended up telling him first thing this morning that we were going to ignore that one small bit of Tradition and meet anyway."

"Cas, you didn't? What'd he say?"

"I did. And you know what? He didn't have anything to say. He did laugh though, loud and long. Once he'd finished, he said that life around the DragonTree Fen was beginning to get interesting."

"Hmmm…I'm not entirely surprised. I like him. And you're sure that's all he said? Nothing negative, no warnings?"

"Not quite all. He did say that if we were going to meet together, we'd better find an out-of-the-way place to do it. He suggested that we meet under the DragonTree."

"That doesn't sound so out-of-the-way," Tuss said suspiciously. He doubted that his new friend Auran would set them up for trouble, though.

"He says it is, and since he patrols that area, he'd be the one to know best. He also said that no one but him goes there, except on very rare occasions."

"Well that's strange. The Tree is the focal point of local dragonfly history. It's the reason we're here at the Fen in the first place, and no one visits it?"

"I thought the same thing, Tuss. But, I like Auran and I trust him too. I told the others and they agreed. We decided that it's where we'd meet. All that is, except for you. So?" The question hung in the air between them.

They stared straight into each other's eyes, the compound facets shimmering with a mixture of blues and greens and reflected whirling patterns.

"Well?"

He was lost in the spinning depths of her gaze, those stunning eyes, so colorful and bright. The effect they had on him was mesmerizing. *They're amazing!* Tuss realized right then that he could look into her eyes for an entire day and be happy. They were very different from those of dragonfly nymphs. Everything about them was different, but looking into those deep pools filled with intelligence, they were very clearly Cas' eyes. He could see that she'd only changed outwardly. She was still Cas, his closest friend and he was filled with joy all over again at their reunion.

"Well?" she asked again.

He looked away from her steady gaze to clear his mind. It worked, though he couldn't quite remember exactly what she'd asked him in the first place. "Well what?"

"Well, are you in? You'll meet with the rest of us tomorrow?"

"Of course I will! I wouldn't miss it for anything."

"Good enough then. I'm hungry, I need to try my wings at hawking again." There was a certain hesitation in her voice.

"You too, huh?" He asked. "It's not as easy as I thought it'd be."

"No it wasn't. I wish that..." She let her voice trail away into silence.

"You wish what?"

"Oh nothing really," she sighed. It was a sad sound.

Tuss noticed that her colors had darkened. Some strong emotion was causing the change and for whatever reason he knew that it meant she was either embarrassed or feeling shy.

"You wish what, Cas?" He pressed for an answer. He thought he knew what she was going to say. He hoped he knew at least.

"I wish everything wasn't so different now, all of the new rules, being alone so much. I'm going to miss being together like we were. So I was just thinking..."

"I know what you mean. I was lonely last night," he agreed quickly.

"I was just thinking that maybe we could hawk together, like the way we used to hunt together, before." She sighed, "I hate that we're supposed to spend the rest of our lives alone. I understand that the Tradition is good and all, but..."

"Me too. I can't believe that we're to just move on now, and leave our friends behind. It's too depressing to think about." He let out a long sigh of regret that matched hers.

"At least there's the meeting tomorrow. We're most definitely breaking the rules then, but I wonder how much of that sort of thing we'll be able to get away with."

"I don't know Cas, we have to wait and see."

"Yeah we'll see, starting tomorrow."

There was a long stretch of time that followed where neither of them wanted to speak or be the first to leave. They were enjoying the companionable silence. Tuss was looking at the great Tree far across the water.

He finally said, "I'll see you tomorrow, Cas."

"Not if I see you first," she shot back quickly.

He pulled his gaze away from the distance and saw that her eyes were agleam. Within that glow was the lovely companion that'd always been there for him. Her gaze was too much. He shyly looked up, sure that his own eyes were giving away how much she affected him. He began to realize again that everything was different and very much the same. They'd changed so much, yet they were still dear friends.

Good! She's still the Castanea I knew and I'm still the Tussilago I was...

He looked again to the south, where the DragonTree stood both in and out of the Fen. His breath froze within him; would he ever get used to the sight of it?

He turned back to say goodbye and saw that Cas had left him silently. He was sorry to see her go.

Oh well, he thought, *I should've asked her if she wanted to go hawking together. Why'd I hesitate?* She was far enough away that he decided to wait for another time. Maybe tomorrow after that meeting.

He continued to watch as she darted all about chasing the tiny insects dragonflies fed upon. She zipped across the surface of the water so quickly, even his amazing new dragonfly eyes could barely keep track.

"Wow! She can really move fast!" He turned away hoping that maybe he could hawk as effectively as she was. He had trouble concentrating on what he was doing though. *Oh well, there's always tomorrow and now tomorrow looks like it's going to be very-very interesting. Oops! I missed another one.*

Hunger eventually drove all other considerations away, and he began to have success. Tuss started to feel sated and realized too, that he was happy and warm inside in a way that he'd never experienced before, and that it wasn't only because he finally had a full stomach.

Chapter Six

Meeting

The next day dawned bright and sunny. As far as Tuss could tell it wasn't any different from either of the last two. The night hadn't been so pleasant. A front had moved in from the west bringing heavy rain with it. Surprisingly, he'd only awakened a couple times due to the bright flashes of lightning and the loud booming thunder. He was decently sheltered within a thick cover of reeds. The pouring rain didn't bother him and he'd stayed dry throughout the entire ordeal.

He knew of the weather changes, but had only experienced them from below the surface. Tuss and his friends had spent many days looking up as the storms passed over the Fen. The noise was tremendous as the water was churned by the pounding of the heavy rain. Occasionally, they'd get nervous, as it seemed to them that the world above was in utter turmoil. They talked about what it was like to actually be out in the storms, unprotected by the comforting layer of the Fen's water.

It bothered Tuss then; the reality, though, wasn't so bad. He told himself, *I did all of that worrying for nothing and what did it get me? I wonder if last night's was a bad one?*

The threat of the storm aside, it was strange and unsettling to perch above the place where the frogs dwelt so thickly. As nymphs it was certain death to wander into the swampy north of the Fen. Frogs were everywhere, their young tadpoles were a great food source and easy prey but the risk of getting to them was too great. Any approach to the frog's spawning grounds put them in peril of becoming a meal themselves. The mature frogs were indifferent about their young but ferocious when it came to their appetites. Dragonfly nymphs seemed to be especially favored by them.

And here Tuss was, perched safely above the reach of even the largest frog with the longest tongue, which struck him as being quite funny. *They were, for so long, a menace from above even just a day or so ago and now they're a menace from below. That's a change I can live with!*

He pulled his mind away from those considerations and focused on the storm free day. It was beautiful and it held a lot of potential. He could feel the promise of exciting things to come, like seeing his friends again, only now, they'd be in their mature forms. That was reason enough but another, more important one would be seeing Cas again. He'd had troubles falling asleep last night because his mind was so full of thoughts of her; that sweet voice and her beautiful new form.

"And of course there are the others," he said happily, trying out his voice, wondering what his friends would think of it. He also wondered how they'd want to approach this new way of life, together or alone. The flying changed everything. The possibilities were infinite. He thought about their diverse personalities. *Will they be different now that they're fliers? Will our relationships really change?*

After the short time spent with Cas, he was confident that she was the same. She was still a natural leader, organizing the meeting proved that much. She'd always been strong-willed and opinionated and yet very easy for him to get along with, most of the time. The two of them were prone to bickering, but they never carried it too far. He thought about how ridiculous it was that silly things could result in absurd amounts of tension. He and Cas were always able to avoid taking every little situation so seriously. They'd never lost control of their tempers with each other or fallen victim to heated exchanges. *I don't know how, though; we're both so determined.*

Coria, was another matter entirely. She was quiet and seldom spoke, usually happy to go along with whatever he and Cas had decided. Only Briza was able to get strong reactions from her. The two of them were so similar when it came to games and competition. She'd always been the best Capture or Hold-The-High-Ground player. Actually she was better at everything, no matter what they played. He wondered if her skills underwater would translate to the world above. He hoped that he'd somehow, someday find out.

Briza, no doubt, will be Briza. Tuss couldn't imagine that he'd change. Loud, generally obnoxious and very good at getting into trouble, that was Briza. Never caring much about what others thought of him, either. The Teachers said he always had an attitude problem. Tuss didn't think the Teachers truly understood his friend. He has a great heart and is endlessly loyal. He just doesn't know how to communicate those qualities in a way that doesn't offend. It was Briza that'd come up with the name *The League* to describe the nine friends when they played in their made-up games. And, when others joined the games, Briza made it very clear that it was the preferred title for only the original nine. It was especially so when they played Capture. When he was teased about it, he'd just shrug it off and say *'it means we're doing something right.'* He wasn't worried about anyone's approval except Tuss' or maybe at times, Cas'. Briza could also be insufferably prideful and vane. *And I bet he spends a lot of time admiring himself in the reflection of the water just as Cas said.*

"We won't be able to live with him." Tuss laughed out loud, enjoying once again how everything sounded so much clearer in the open air.

Standoff

The sounds, the sights, everything; it was all so distinct now.

Tuss thought of Gal, sure that he'd be the one to try and explain why everything looked so much clearer with their new eyes. Gal was the curious one, always interested in new knowledge and understanding. Tuss considered how to describe his thoughtful friend; *Gal's the thinker, the smart one, curious and inquisitive.* He somehow knew more about the up above world than should have been possible. Gal's mind was intuitive. He was able to extrapolate and theorize with abilities that were almost prescient. It was scary. Tuss couldn't wait to hear what Gal thought about all of the changes they'd gone though. He was sure that his thoughtful friend would have more to say when there was time to hear.

Talking too much, which wouldn't be a problem with Leon who was a lot like Coria in that he seldom spoke up unless first prompted by one of the others. That was okay with Tuss since having a few quiet members in their group was a good thing. He knew that there was no guile in Leon's silence. He was a stalwart friend, reliable, trustworthy and faithful. His nature was peaceable, steady and calm. He wasn't easy to upset, even the worst of Briza's foibles left him unfazed. Tuss would describe him as self contained. Leon liked being part of the group, but it didn't seem like he needed to be part of a group. He was second only to Aneth in size and capability.

To say that Aneth was the strength of the group was an understatement. He was almost twice the size of any of them, except for Leon and Gal. He was strongest by far, and his physical attributes carried over into his personality. Aneth was self assured and fearless but never a bully. He was a gentle giant as a nymph, never one to ridicule another for being weaker or smaller. *Aneth is as sweet natured as he is big. I think that's what I like most about him.* Tuss had never seen him using his size, strength or physical abilities to gain any unfair advantage over another. None of the friends could ask for a better friend, one that was as strong, dependable and best of all, peaceable.

Of the nine that were supposed to be at the meeting, Mira was the one that Tuss knew the least about. She was a puzzle; small, fast, quiet and hard to define. He knew that she could be counted on, the very essence of reliability. She was almost as quiet as Leon, although Tuss had heard Mira and Ace talk up a storm together. The two were very close when they were nymphs. They paired off well together when they played Capture and they undoubtedly would still be close as mature dragonflies. It made perfect sense since they were so much alike. Ace was the more social of the two and actively involved herself in whatever it was the friends were getting themselves into. Ace wasn't afraid to let herself be heard and she didn't back down if she knew she was on the right side of an issue.

As thoughts of the two females finished running through his mind, Tuss realized that he'd arrived at the DragonTree. He passed from sunlight into shadow, swooping down to the surface and pulled up just short of his final destination. He hovered in place, positioned under the farthest-reaching branches of the DragonTree. Beams of sunlight penetrated through its canopy and cast a strange glow all around, creating an otherworldly atmosphere. The same light scattered off the Fen's surface and shimmered with myriads of ever changing shapes and shadows. The water danced in crazy ripples, the wind blew the branches of the great Tree. The combination sent reflections bouncing everywhere. The effect was hypnotic, nearly too much for Tuss' mind to take in. His eyes were dazzled.

There was no way to describe this place more in depth. His kind, the dragonflies of DragonTree had found something that was truly special indeed. *And to think we've been here for generation after generation!*

Tuss was struck again with fresh wonder. *What a world we live in!*

Feeling like an invader, he finally flew deeper into the natural enclosure. He was moving slowly, looking to see if anyone else had arrived ahead of him. They had. He could hear voices. One of them he knew already. It belonged to Cas. It was as sweet sounding as he remembered. There were a couple others that sounded distinct, maybe a little familiar but he knew that it'd be hard to guess which voice went with which friend.

Well, that deep one seems obvious enough; it has to be Aneth's. It's near enough to the way he sounded underwater. Tuss flew a little closer, moving slowly, enjoying the moment. His new-old friends were speaking excitedly, talking over one another. Hearing it this way, so like before and yet very different, reminded him of all of the changes that'd taken place in just a few short days. And changes or not, the overall cacophony of the group was enough like before to make him feel that old sense of belonging to something larger than himself. The bunch of noisy creatures gathered together under the DragonTree, were most definitely his friends. The rhythm and cadences of their speech, their interactions. *Yeah, no doubt, it's them.*

And then he finally saw them.

Tuss was overtaken with feelings of friendship and community. He knew that he belonged, that he was meant to be with these lovely creatures and that no matter what else happened, he wanted to spend as much time in their company as was possible.

But that's not how it's supposed to go. A strong sense of loss replaced his initial joy at seeing his friends. *I hardly knew how alone I was feeling the last two days!*

Seeing them for the very first time, changed as they were, Tuss knew they'd find a way to honor their Tradition and yet still live together in one form or another. Satisfied with the idea, but not quite ready to fly right in and announce his arrival, he decided to hover and watch a while longer. There was so much going on inside of him, putting off the reunion for just a bit couldn't hurt.

"There you are!"

Tuss was startled by the closeness of Cas' voice. His quiet time of observation and reverie was over.

"Hi Cas!" he replied. All eyes were on him now. "I was trying to take everything in. You were right, this place is really special."

The shouts of "Tuss" from the others drowned out the last of what he was trying to say. He was caught up in a whirlwind of wings and excited voices. He joined in the madness. All nine of the friends were zipping about in the flickering light under the sweeping branches. They were showing off to one another, more so to him, demonstrating their new abilities and sleek new forms. Once they'd calmed down from their excitement and quieted enough for everyone to hear Cas speak, re-introductions were made.

When all was said and done, Tuss could hardly believe how perfectly each of his friends' new forms fit their personalities. Coria was a burning-red Autumn Candleflame, small in size but sleek and fast looking. Gal, a Twelve-Spot had a light blue body and immense wings with black and white patches marking them. Mira, an Eastern Amberwing was small, burnt-orange and had matching wings, patched in browns and yellows that nearly glowed in the shadows. Ace was a Calico Pennant, the same size as Mira but dark red and black along her body. She had red saddles and black spots on her wings with bright red highlights. Leon was a Great Blue Dasher, appearing much like Tuss and Cas, only larger and darker with white spangles on his wings. Briza the Banded Pennant, sleek and angular with wildly black patterned wings and a pale blue body, was smaller than the other males but probably much faster. And then there was Aneth, the most impressive of all. He was a Dragonhunter Clubtail, huge, powerful, colored black, yellow and green. Tuss wondered if he'd ever meet another who's stature so impressed him.

He concluded that, *Yeah, they absolutely have forms and colors that match their personalities which is simply amazing!*

"Okay, should we get started?" Cas asked.

"Yes!" chorused everyone.

"Isn't that why we're here?" Briza fired back, "I mean, to get started? But, what exactly are we getting started?"

"I don't have a plan or anything quite like that, Briza. I just thought that we could, you know, figure things out once we were together." Cas sounded flustered. Briza's abrupt nature had that effect on everyone.

"Hey Briza, it's only day three, take it easy," Aneth said, his voice deep and rumbling. "I'm happy enough to be here with the rest of you. What's it matter if we don't have a reason beyond just seeing each other?"

"Okay, Aneth's right. You know me, Cas, I run off at the mouth. No offense intended."

"None taken Briza. I did want us to meet just for the sake of it mostly, but I also..." She paused and then blurted out in a rush, "I also wanted to ask everyone if this was really it? Are we really going to go our separate ways? Are we going to forget the closeness we had before? Do we go along with that aspect of the Tradition just because we're maturing dragonflies now?"

There was a long silence in which uncomfortable looks were exchanged.

Tuss saw that no one wanted to be the first to speak up. Even Briza, to his utter amazement, seemed to be unwilling to say anything. He was impressed that Cas was willing to say what everyone else seemed reluctant to.

"Ummm, for me, that'd be a big no way! And that's to every question you just asked. Seeing everyone today, I've no intention to keep all to myself," Tuss finally said.

Everyone made it all too clear that they agreed.

Tuss continued, "It's only been three days and two nights and I don't even know when I'm supposed to start being mature or where or even how. It's all supposed to be explained somehow by the Tradition but has anyone told any of you where you belong? How or where you should find your area?" He could see the answers in their eyes, "no" prevailed. "Auran told me that the north end was open, so that's where I've stayed the last two nights."

"Same here," Cas agreed. "He also said that we could contend for any particular spot we liked well enough, but..."

"Oh dear! I'd never do that on purpose!" A high, but pretty sounding voice said. It was Coria's. "I thought someone would be showing us where we should patrol and where we were to live." Her voice changed as she said, "and just like Tuss, I don't want to be alone."

"Me either Coria. We should all take Auran's advice about looking in the north. You know, try to move into the same area. There's certainly enough room for all of us, am I right Tuss?" Cas asked.

"There's plenty of room. I didn't see a single dragonfly anywhere near the reeds I perched on. I'm sure all of you could find places there. It'd be great to know you were close by." Tuss was excited by the idea that his friends would be living and patrolling near him. "When the sun came up I flew all over the area. No one was moving but me. I've never felt so isolated. Except," he paused, reluctant to broach what he knew would be the one catch.

"Except," Gal knew Tuss too well. His voice was colored with humor. "Except what Tussilago? I know by the tone of your voice, something's amiss."

"Frogs, it's the north, remember. The area is infested with them."

Voices began to rise in protest and chagrin but before the complaints got out of control, Tuss did his best to quiet them by continuing, "The reeds in the area are tall, huge actually. I was able to perch safely only half way up their height; that put me high above danger and still kept me sheltered overhead. The frogs were no threat from below, the bats were no threat from above. I stayed dry during the storm. I don't know why the region is so empty of our kind."

"That's simple enough, we're too few to fill the shoreline of a body of water the Fen's size," Gal said. "The dangers you mentioned don't' worry me, I'll join you Tuss. As always, I trust your judgment. You haven't led us wrong as yet."

"Frogs, bats, storms, whatever! That's just more opportunity for action and adventure, I'm in," agreed Briza. "I told Cas two days ago and I'll say it again today. I don't want to be alone. It's only been three days and I'm already bored half out of my mind. I can't stop thinking about what it will be like weeks from now. If nothing changes I'll go crazy. I need others to talk to."

"You're already crazy Briza, we just haven't told you yet. And having you talk to us on daily basis is likely to make the rest of us crazy," Gal said.

Briza spun towards him ready with an angry reply. His colors had darkened and he looked fearsome, almost scary. Gal was laughing at his reaction.

"Why you..."

"You didn't tell me that, Briza. I wish you had, though," Cas said, interrupting before Briza said something that would start a pointless argument.

"I didn't?" Briza's anger faded into puzzlement.

"No, you didn't!" She allowed exasperation to color her reply.

"Well, I meant too. Maybe I was so excited to see everyone I forgot.

But that doesn't matter so much now. What does though, is what you said."

"Oh?" She sounded genuinely curious.

"Yeah, and I agree. I can't see us following the Tradition the way it's expected of us."

"I'm with you there," said Coria. "Yesterday I nearly got into several fights with larger dragonflies, simply by flying into the wrong places and I've no way of knowing where the right places are. It hardly seems fair." Her voice fell to what was almost a whisper, "and I spent most of last night awake, wishing that I was safe, back underwater with the rest of you. I love flying, but I love all of you more. I can't stand the idea of living alone. It's awful!"

Everyone agreed.

"That's how I found her yesterday," Cas said, looking at Coria. "She was ready to take on a huge Comet Darner. She was in his area, but there she was, bright red, angry and only one fourth his size. Our raging Coria."

"Yeah, I don't think I'd have come out of that one too well, your timing was perfect Cas, thanks again!"

"Don't mention it Coria," Cas laughed a little, "and you're welcome to trespass in my area, when I get one, anytime. Okay?"

"Okay!"

"Can we get back on subject?" Leon interrupted. His voice was mellow and quiet and surprised everyone. He didn't assert himself very often, at least not before emergence.

Tuss looked closer at his changed friend, impressed.

Leon wasn't finished speaking either. "Tuss, Cas, if you say there's space enough, I'd love to situate myself near you. I imagine Mira would come along too?" He looked questioningly at her.

"Oh yes, certainly. If that's the best solution, then count me in. I'm happy with whatever everybody decides." It was the first time Tuss had heard her speak without the competing noise of others. She had a dusky voice.

"Ace, what about you?" asked Cas.

"What Mira and Leon said works just fine with me," Ace answered. Tuss liked the way her red and black colors contrasted in the shimmering reflections bouncing off the water. "It'll be fun living close together like before."

Gal hadn't spoken since teasing a reaction out of Briza. "It's the most logical thing for us to do, living close together. Assuming your impressions of the place are accurate Tuss, we will be far away from the heart of the Fen. I like that, isolated, but not alone." His voice took on a conspiratorial tone; "I explored that area extensively yesterday, especially where the great reed beds of the northern swamps begin. I'm curious about what lies beyond. It'll be easier to satisfy that curiosity with fewer strangers looking on."

Tuss liked what he was hearing; his friends seemed to want the same things. "There's a decent mud bank there on the Fen side of the reeds with plenty of ground cover and tall plants. They stopped most of the wind that blew in with last night's storm. I wasn't in any danger of being blown off my perch since they overhang enough. Actually as I mentioned before I was quite dry and comfortable. And best of all, there's plenty of room to spare."

"Gal, what'd you just..."

"Yeah Gal," Briza spoke over Cas, "you planning to do some exploring?"

Gal's eyes flashed, contrasting greatly with his dark gray body. "That's not what matters at the moment Briza, you haven't given an answer yet, you haven't either, Aneth."

"He's right," Cas agreed. "What's it going to be you two?"

74

"Oh, I had a choice in the matter? The rest of you seem to have decided already and I said I didn't want to be alone. And, not that anyone listens to me anyway. I already said I'm in."

"Calm down Briza, we didn't conspire or anything. You've been here through the entire conversation."

"I'm calm. But I..."

"Next time," she spoke up loudly overtopping his rant, "we need to discuss living arrangements we'll remember to ask for your opinion first, all right?"

"Oh suuure, whatever!" he knew he was being teased. "Considering how things went this time, I hope to get the first pick when we get up there. Especially, since I was about the last one asked." When no one responded, he went on. "Oh, I'm not joking. In fact, I may even choose the spot Tuss has already claimed. That's if it suits my tastes and particular needs."

"I'm not so sure I like that idea." Tuss had grown fond of his spot. "You'll have a challenge on your wings."

Briza cut him off, "I'm joking, Tuss. I don't care where I land as long as I can stay out of reach from the sticky frog tongues, avoid attacks from birds and bats and get out of the heavy rain now and then. Keep your spot, but help me find a good one."

"The same old Briza," Coria said. "Can't take the teasing and can't make it clear when he's teasing."

"Hey I was born me and that's what I have to be," he said slyly.

"Not all of the time, I hope," Cas said with the perfect touch of chagrin in her voice.

He preened on his perch, the ideal picture of mischief.

"As I said, same old Briza," Coria repeated.

"Nicely said, Coria. I couldn't put it better myself," Aneth finally spoke.

"Yeah, yeah," Briza said lightheartedly. "What about you Aneth? You haven't answered yet."

"I'll go where Tuss and Cas go, and will be happy that the rest of you will be there as well."

"That's it then. We're all agreed," Cas said happily. "So what else do we need to discuss?"

When none of them had anything to say, Aneth spoke again. "It seems to me that we came here to discuss us."

"You're going to have to explain that one. We're going to discuss, *us*?"

"Yes Briza, us. To put it simply, we now know that we're still who we were but don't know exactly what we're to be. So yeah, let's talk about us. We need to discuss what we want, what we expect from tomorrow and what we do next."

"Who can argue with that?" Briza said with a laugh.

When no one did, they began to get to know each other all over again.

***

They stayed together and chatted for hours about what they'd seen and how they'd felt and everything that happened since their emergence. Every one of them had something to add to the discussion. Mid-day passed into afternoon, and nothing, or no one disturbed them the entire time.

None of them noticed the big, graying dragonfly that looked in on them now and again. None knew that a guardian, a friendly spectator was watching over them.

Observing the nine, Auran could imagine a better future for their kind. The small community that was forming with these peculiar friends was exhilarating. He knew that he'd done the right thing by encouraging them to gather together. He was glad that Cas and Tuss had detected his not-so-subtle hints. He was happy that he'd played a small part in bringing about what he was seeing.

***

After a while, Tuss noticed that Cas was separated from the group. He flew over to her to ask if everything was okay.

"Hey Cas. How are you doing?" he asked.

"Oh I'm fine. Just fine," she answered quietly.

"Are you sure? You sound a little, ummm, funny?"

"Yeah, I'm fine Tuss, really I am," she assured him. "But just a day ago, I didn't think I'd ever be this happy again. I was afraid that things wouldn't work out."

"It does seem like things will work out, doesn't it?"

"Uh-huh. I'm pretty sure that everything's going to be okay." She looked at him with those deep whirling eyes. "Won't it?"

Those beautiful, depthless, multifaceted eyes; he was lost in them for a time. "Yes," he finally said, "it'll be okay."

He looked away from her, back at the happy group. "I think that things are going to be grand, wonderful, exciting and not least of all, interesting."

Cas and Tuss rejoined the others. They continued to talk about their new world and its possibilities. And, as they talked, they grew closer together. '*Everything is going to be just fine*' was how Cas had put it at some point in the conversation. It was during a lull and all of them agreed; they knew exactly what she was talking about.

***

Everything was not okay for DragonTree Fen, however. The spies of Hive watched the nine from the shadows and, as they did, hate grew stronger within their shared mind.

They are not Hive, they are not Legion, they do not belong together and they will pay for the mockery.

The group-mind, controlled by Third, was in accord; the contemptuous creatures must be eliminated. The spies would not attack until commanded. The Imperative pulsed within them; the time would come soon enough. *Hive will conquer, Hive will rule...*

They had gathered enough information. They left the Fen in secret, following the path that Second's cohort had taken days before. Their destination was Hive, their fetid home, sinking ever more deeply into decay.

Third reached out across the great distance and briefly touched the Queen's disturbed thoughts. She brooded as she waited for more input. The mind Third touched was drowsy, corrupt and chaotic. Her news would make little sense to the failing matriarch. The Queen's struggle to keep the nightmarish dreams at bay was never ending, and drove her mad.

Third withdrew her querying search even as Second's cohort arrived.

As Second approached, large warrior drones buzzed about the entrance, blocking access to all lacking Hive's social pheromone signature.

Approved, she proceeded deep into the rotting ruin.

The chambers of the hollow log were covered with fungi and clusters of slimy, fetid mushrooms. Every surface oozed thick, toxic fluids and noxious gases, the combination of which corrupted body and mind.

The Queen's small, inner niche glowed with a surreal, greenish light.

She was present in body but lost in mind.

Second departed, her report not given. The Queen was unresponsive. The Imperative-implanted pulsed, her minions responded and went about their daily tasks, every one, Second included; a slave to the command structure.

The Queen stirred after her sub-queen exited

I cannot see what I must see...I feel nothing that I should feel...but I must find a way, Swarm, our dread enemy of old, them that cast me off is encroaching, the conquest is near begun but I can't...

Her eyes glazed over as her once great physical strength failed again. The toxins from the glowing fungi had long ago entered her body's life sustaining systems. Her exhausted mind began to wander the grotesque, poisoned nightmares that were the birthplace of her rage against all living beings. In the past it was only Swarm that attracted the Queens voracious attention. The two colonies were diverse creatures, the bees of Hive and the wasps of Swarm, always at odds, fighting an endless war. Was the Queen the only capable fighter? That was possible, she being the only wasp amongst bees. She was after all originally of Swarm, an invading usurper of the bee queen. Hive was consistently coming out on the losing side. With every successive defeat, the Queen slipped ever deeper into her hate-fueled insanity.

The Watchers

Chapter Seven

Sunny Days and Long Thoughts

Tuss was a speeding streak of blue as he flashed through the bright sunlight. He swerved hard and began to dive, moving so fast the world was a blur of colors that he was passing through. He found, to his surprise, that he was in the forefront. He'd never been able to out fly Coria before. Any who tried in the past weeks ended up looking foolish.

Is that it? An accident. I wasn't trying and it just happened.

Tuss was faster than most of his kind, but not Coria, not until this very moment. Dashers had a reputation for speed; they were very plain to look at, but fast on the wing. Coria was faster still. She was the best of them in flight, quicker and more maneuverable. Only Briza, on occasion, had been able to keep up with her, until today.

Tuss felt a surge of joy, as he sped onwards, nothing between him and the horizon. As he went, he couldn't help but think, *I'm glad that I caught Coria off guard. I doubt I'd have much hope of out-flying her for long otherwise.*

The friends hadn't organized any specific activity for the day. They'd just been flying around, enjoying each other's company, when on a whim Tuss had flown past Coria, *tagging* her in the process. He called out a teasing challenge, laughing as he poured on speed.

"See if you can catch me this time!"

She didn't hesitate and neither did the others. On a day like this, everyone was in the mood for fun.

Tuss flew as hard as he could, laughing loudly, happy to be alive and with his closest friends in raucous pursuit. He was about to turn and cast another taunt back over his wings, when he felt something lightly brushing his back.

"You're it!" A small red body passed just over his head, picking up speed as it went. It was Coria and she mimicked his laugh as she disappeared around a patch of reeds. His eyes could barely keep up. *Oh well! It was fun while it lasted.*

What started out as an impromptu game amongst the group of them quickly turned into a full-blown melee of follow-the-leader or, in this case, tag-the-leader. As Tuss chased after Coria, he noticed that there were far more than nine dragonflies careening their way through the reedy thickets. Apparently, others had seen what was going on and decided to join in. All of it unplanned, and a complete surprise to everyone. Nobody asked to be included, they saw the fun the nine were having and wanted to be part of it. Not even the irascible Briza minded. He'd even flown by Tuss at one point shouting something about, "The more the merrier, more for me to..." The rest was lost in his increasingly disturbing laughter.

Tuss pulled up out of the noisy stream of sleek, speeding bodies, gained a little altitude and stopped for a good look at what was happening. He was astounded. A large group of dragonflies, all of them shouting, screaming, taunting and laughing, having fun and most obviously, not worried about heeding the Tradition's suggestion of isolation, were having the time of their young lives.

I hardly know what to think of it all!

Tuss tried to count, but quickly lost track, as more excited newcomers joined in. There was no way possible to follow the action. The game of tag had turned into a chaotic whirlwind of dragonflies going every which way. The sight of so many different kinds was a marvel to behold. He saw that for most of them, it didn't even matter exactly who was supposed to be chasing whom. As the game continued to grow in numbers, it moved from the northeast corner of the Fen and over into the east meadows.

No one had stopped the proceedings to suggest they move. As a group they naturally progressed the center of activity elsewhere. The meadows were the perfect location for what was happening. The danger of misjudging height and speed and accidentally flying straight into the water, which meant certain death, was eliminated.

Tuss could also see that the tall grasses and brushy scrubs added variety and challenge, whereas the reeds and open water limited possibilities. Ideas began to fill his head, exciting, interesting ideas. *That's for later. For now, I'm going to have some fun.* Tuss quit his hover and dove into the maelstrom of flying chaos.

The merriment lasted until the first hungry birds, attracted by the ruckus arrived. Shouts and screams of warning from all around sent the players in too-dizzying-to-follow swoops and spirals. The fun and games had turned all too serious. Dragonflies instinctively maneuvered in evasive patterns. They transitioned naturally, they were born to hunt and apparently they were born to survive as well. The sheer numbers of darting, flashing and speeding bodies confused the birds so badly, they quickly became confounded.

Tuss watched as one Shadow Darner, late to react to the threat, made it to the cover of a thick bush just before a pursuing bird. Heedless of where it was, the bird crashed headlong into the very spot the Darner easily passed through, evoking laughter from the escapee's friends.

How they find a close call like that so funny is beyond me.

After many failed attempts, the birds left the meadow in search for prey that required less effort. Once the black and menacing flock was gone, the players made a head-count. None came up missing. Briza blustered and joked that their kind was far superior on the wing, therefore the birds posed no threat. As he was bragging, someone did their best to imitate the squawk of one of the departed predators. Briza's reaction garnered much laughter. He angrily flew about trying to find the culprit. Tuss was certain that real violence would commence if he was successful. The joker was wise enough to remain anonymous and no one else was foolish enough to give them up to the raging Briza.

Coria was able to calm him down. She reminded him of his many underwater pranks, some of which bordered on the cruel. She must've whispered about one in particular that pleased him, Tuss couldn't hear which it was, but Briza started laughing and the *crisis* was narrowly avoided. She looked towards Tuss with a mixture of relief and upset in her eyes. Later she would tell him that she hated Briza's prankish nature and equally hated using his past *successes* in that arena to placate him. Tuss wondered if the whole ordeal was a portent of trouble to come. Briza had gotten very excited even to the point of out-of-control during the simple game they'd been playing.

Once calm was restored there came calls for restarting the play that was interrupted by the bird invasion. Those calls were few, however. Most could see that the day was darkening as the sun started to sink low on the western horizon. Dozens of laughing dragonflies, their near death experiences forgotten, headed back to the Fen, ready to get some serious hawking in before the evening became too cool and dark. The new players were breaking up into small groups, many, planning for the first time, to work together for the hunt.

Tuss shouted out before they were too widely spread out, "Hey! Everyone!" Dozens of whirling eyes turned his way, "why don't we meet back here tomorrow, in the meadow I mean, and do it all over again?"

He was answered with a loud cheer of agreement.

Narrow Escape

"I can hardly believe what happened," Cas said sighing with tired contentment.

"Same here. That was the most fun I've had since we emerged," Briza said. "Aside from the idiot that..."

"You mean, aside from the birds." Cas made a squawking sound.

"No I don't mean that, Cas!" Briza started to fly off.

"Briza! Let it go, someone got the better of you. Deal with it for once," Gal said.

Briza stopped and whirled around angrier than ever.

Aneth spoke quickly, "Think clearly before you speak, Briza. None of us want you to leave in a huff. Remember how that turned out last time? It took you how long to discover that we're the best you're ever going to get, friend-wise that is?"

Briza flew back towards them without answering. He was clearly struggling to control his emotions. The others let him be for a time, hoping he'd reason things out peacefully.

"So, where were we?" Tuss asked after the silence stretched for an uncomfortable time.

"We were talking about having fun, Tuss. Except, the birds."

"That's it. We need to figure out what to do about them if we're going to keep playing in the open."

"You mean, set up a watch or something?"

"Just that Coria. And a signal too. Something that no one will forget or misunderstand."

"That'll work! I like all three ideas; playing, keeping a watch and a signal," Aneth said.

Ace and Mira chorused, "Me, too!"

"What have we started here?" Cas asked, as they headed back from the long day of play.

"I'm not sure Cas, but I'm not at all sorry about it, even considering the birds. And think about this, we could try and get a real game of Capture going tomorrow, a big one!"

"That's an interesting thought, Tuss," said Gal. "A lot of the rules and principles from before will have to change, but we can make the adjustments. What do you say to that, Briza?"

Briza must have dealt with his anger and laid it to rest. He answered as his normal self, "I think that we better get to it quickly and figure it all out tonight. I hope that it's as fun on the wing as it was underwater."

"Me too, I can't wait! But we have to be safe, more thoughtful and better prepared for danger." Coria sounded excited.

The friends talked right up until dark, and even then, had a tough time departing to their separate perches for the night. There was so much to think about, so much fun to be had. Rest would elude all of them until very late.

***

They got started early the next morning. No one had slept soundly. First, it was patrols and hawking. All of them wanted a good meal for starters and they had their responsibilities to fulfill. It was one thing to break from the Tradition by playing games, which was harmless, but another to ignore what was unquestionably their obligation to their home and their kind.

"Who could complain about this arrangement?" Briza asked as they headed out across the Fen, their duties finished. The meadow was before them, green and blazing in the late morning sunlight.

"Yeah, we've kept the Tradition and now we have the rest of the day to ourselves," Cas said happily.

"Ourselves?" Briza huffed. "Did you forget about the dozens of others that'll be joining us, Cas?"

"Oh, right! Thanks for the reminder, Mister Obvious."

"Hey! I didn't say it was a bad thing!"

"Same old Briza," Coria teased. "Let's see if you can keep your temper and fly any better than you argue." She swiped past him, yelled *'tag'* and darted away, disappearing around a large boulder. He chased Gal, Leon, Mira and Ace just a wing-beat behind.

Tuss and Cas hung back for a moment, watching.

"After you?" Tuss finally asked.

Cas looked him in the eyes, laughed and then tagged him on the side. Her wings beat the air and her laughing voice answered with, "Yeah! After me!"

***

And so it began.

One day faded into the next, as the eastern meadows became the focus for the young dragonflies so recently emerged from the Fen's cold embrace. Most had been friends and acquaintances when they were nymphs. A lot of them had played games of underwater Capture together. Tuss and company, inventors of the games, had unknowingly left behind their own special kind of Tradition. This new form of interaction simply felt like a natural transition for all the nymphs that emerged after them.

***

On a day like any other, like lightning from the blue, the three Elders of DragonTree showed up. Their *mission* was to inform the newly emerged that the northern regions of the Fen were the most likely place for them to find open areas to settle into. They also had said some

88

words about the Tradition, isolation and responsibility.

"Well duh!" Mira said after the visit. "It's not like we needed to hear that now that we've been up here for nearly a full moon phase."

"I wonder what they think we've been doing all of this time?" Briza's question went unanswered. What was there to say? They had a good laugh, though.

The fun in the eastern meadows continued, and despite the resentment of being told the obvious by the late arriving Elders, the friends realized that, while the north part of the Fen wasn't as nice in some ways, it was better in many others. The little flying insects their kind fed upon swarmed in large quantities around the swampy regions. It took very little time and energy to hawk. That advantage alone left them with more time to spend together. Life was settling into a nice steady rhythm. Each day blended into the next. There were long stretches where no one noticed that time was moving on at all. The days passed by uncounted.

***

Eventually, Tuss began to feel less contented with how every day felt the same. He loved the life he lived and the friends he shared it with, but something was missing and he had no clue what that something was. *I won't get any real peace of mind until I do.*

He was flying high, part of a prearranged attack pattern. His Wing included Briza, Cas and a slightly older dragonfly named Thymus. A *Wing* was a small group of players organized for one purpose or another and there could be many Wings per team. Thymus had been the first of the older dragonflies to join in the games, but he certainly wasn't the last. More and more of the older ones joined every day. The draw of the games was too great a temptation for most of the Fen's residents to resist.

Tuss' Wing was about to fly into action. Everything was set up perfectly, the pre-game plan was playing out just like they'd hoped it would. The one problem was that Tuss' restless mind kept distracting him. *What are we doing here?* That first thought, clearer than anything he'd considered lately led to others. *Is this all there is? Playing games or living alone? Isn't the world bigger than the Fen, the DragonTree and the east meadows? Do we have a greater purpose?*

The questions kept coming; they flooded his mind.

"Tuss, is everything okay?" Thymus asked, startling him from his thoughts.

"COME ON!" shouted Briza, "We have them. They've taken the bait, don't stop now!"

"Go without me," Tuss shouted to them as he slowed to a hover. "There's something that I need to do, something I need to think through." The flood continued, feelings, ideas, the beginning of understanding. The nagging issues that'd been tugging at his heart and mind for weeks needed answers.

"WAIT! WHAT! NOW! HUH! Are you crazy! Right when we're about to win? Are you crazy?" Briza sounded surprised, agitated and excited all at the same time.

"Yeah I'm crazy, thanks Briza! Thymus, please take over for me, would you? You can lead the Wing as well, if not better, than I can anyway."

"Will do Tuss, thanks."

"There are times I can't figure you out, Tussilago," Briza began.

"Thanks Thymus." Tuss looked at Briza, "It's just a game and there'll be plenty more for us to play. Go on, beat them and then tell me about it later."

"BAH!" Briza shouted back as he turned to catch up with the others. He joined Thymus in leading them towards the *enemy* positions.

Tuss flew away from the center of activity, looking for a quiet spot to think. He was sure that his team would successfully capture the chosen spot and win the match without him. It would probably be Coria who actually got to the objective and finished the capture. She usually did.

Their team, their *League* as Briza insisted on calling them, never lost. A quick look at the confused and broken formations of the enemy showed Tuss all he needed to know about this particular match. His abandonment wouldn't hurt them; he'd feel no guilt.

He flew over to the edge of the meadow and landed on a sunny outcropping of rocks. It was one that'd been used several times in the past for the games. He chose the highest spot with the best lines of site, told one of the restless lookouts that he'd take over his responsibilities and settled in. He'd be able to watch for birds and see events unfold as he pondered all that'd just flashed through his mind.

Hmmm, now what's been missing, he kept repeating to himself. He lost all track of time and, soon enough, forgot to pay any attention to the game. He even forgot to watch the skies; fortunately the harassing birds were busy elsewhere. He didn't even notice his friends as they came one by one to perch nearby. They joined him as they were tagged out or as their part to play was finished.

Briza and Coria were the last of the nine to arrive.

"She did it again!" Briza's voice broke through Tuss' reflections. He sounded happy and excited.

Tuss knew that the game had gone well, Briza's cheerful tone spoke volumes.

"Once again, the League is the victor and Coria is our champion. You should've seen her, Tuss!"

"Briza! You're embarrassing me and everyone knows that I'm the one that got the capture because the rest of the team made it possible.

I'm nothing special. It's the rest of you that make it work." She sounded proud but simultaneously humble.

"Don't be so modest. You're the best player out here, Coria. Sure, we all work together and do our best, but it's your amazing abilities that make the difference."

"Briza!" Cas said, her tone hard. "Let it go, okay?"

"Alright! I just wish that I could fly half as good." He looked at the others, "She deserves all the praise we can give her."

Aneth's deep voice rumbled in agreement, "You really are the best, Coria. We're lucky you're on our team. Briza has a big mouth, but that doesn't mean that everything he says is wrong."

"Oh great! Pick on poor Briza when he's trying to..."

"And," Cas said, cutting him off before he could get going, "we're even more fortunate to have you as a friend. Right?"

"Oh yeah, right, that too," Briza replied quickly. Wanting to avoid one of Cas' lectures he added, "You're one of the best of friends too!"

Good! Tuss thought. *I'm not in the mood for an argument.*

"They almost had us there, Tuss. Why'd you fly out of the game? You disappeared. You aren't hurt are you? What happened?" asked Cas.

"Well, uh," Tuss wanted to answer, but he didn't know which question he should address first.

"He started thinking," Briza said, giving everyone a knowing look, cutting Tuss off before he could begin.

"Oh! That again?" Cas asked.

"Yes, it was that again, but I had another excuse too," Tuss said, a little defensively. "I relieved one of the lookouts. He was crazy with impatience and wanted nothing more than to play. So, here I am, supposedly keeping a watch out for birds, not doing a very good job at it though, and thinking."

"What was it this time? There were no shouts of *Break-break!* So you're off the hook for inattention and by the way, that was a brilliant idea Gal."

"Thanks," he replied. It was Gal that suggested they have a standard call that was for emergencies only. They settled on *"Break-Break!"* They all agreed that it would only be used in the direst of circumstances and never, aiming this rule at Briza, used as a ploy or ruse to trick another team.

Cas picked up right where she left off, "Or is it something you aren't planning to tell us?"

"Oh, it's nothing new really."

"Nothing new? You were willing to risk our first loss over nothing?" Briza didn't sound angry or upset, as Tuss would've expected; he sounded concerned. "I know it had to be more than just nothing. Come on now, what gives?"

Tuss looked at Briza. He didn't see any reproach in his friend's eyes. They mirrored the concern in his voice. It wasn't often that he'd seen that kind of emotion coming from Briza. Tuss looked at Cas, and what he saw in her eyes gave him the assurance that it was safe to speak his thoughts and feelings. He could see that she'd listen to whatever it was that he needed to say. Her support was a gift freely given.

"Okay then! I was thinking about how life's been lately. How every new day goes pretty much like the one before, how nothing changes that much." He paused and laughed a little. *Hmmm, that was a pretty good start.*

He saw his friends begin to relax. He wondered what it was they'd expected to hear him say. *They must've thought that something really bad was going on inside of me.*

"Go on, Tuss," Cas urged.

"This has got to be the very best way to live, right? I mean, we spend every day together and we're never far from one another during the nights. No one has told us what to do, aside from the vague and very rare hints and suggestions we get.

"Well, there was that one time."

"Hush Briza, let him speak," Coria scolded.

Tuss continued. "You know the ones I mean, the stuff we hear from some of the older, more stoic dragonflies. And that one visit, as Briza just reminded us, from the Elders. Right?"

"Yeah Coria, right?" Briza said smugly.

Aneth grumbled, telling him to be quiet. The others agreed with him.

Briza answered them with a surly, "What'd I do?" and then finally quieted.

"Anyway, here we are," Tuss continued again, hoping that Briza would keep quiet long enough for him to finish. "We have an entire world stretching out all around us, in every direction, and it's filled with all kinds of places to explore. There's so much to see and do and there are all kinds of creatures to meet. I know that sounds strange, but think about it; we're surrounded by them." Tuss' voice filled with wonder as he spoke, and it began to affect his friends, "I was thinking about the Butterflies, the Grasshoppers, the Antlions and the Mantids, all of the other creatures that can fly. Just imagine the possibilities, how many there are and how different from us they are. And that's not to mention the ones that don't fly; there must be thousands."

"You want to meet them? All of them?" asked Mira. "But why?"

"What are Mantids, Tuss? I haven't seen any of those yet, at least I don't think so," Ace said.

"You'd know if you saw one," Gal answered for him. "That's if you lived through the encounter. They have a nasty reputation. They like to eat our kind, if and when possible."

"Yuck!" Ace replied, "You want to get to know them, Tuss?"

"I'm with her Tuss, why?" Cas asked.

"Why not?" He shot back quickly, regretting his sharp tone. He quieted and looked at them, avoiding Cas' eyes.

Gal wasn't satisfied with the simple reply. "You'll need to clarify a bit more, Tuss. Mantids are dangerous and my impression is that the butterflies tend to be terribly unfriendly. They barely acknowledge that we exist. I tried to approach one once to ask if it minded the time we spend in the meadows."

"You did? When was that?" Cas asked.

"Just a couple of days after we moved the games over to here. These meadows are more or less their place. I was trying to be polite."

"Oh! I didn't think about doing that. What a nice thing to do, Gal."

"Thanks, Cas, but I doubt it did any good. It just flew away as if I didn't exist. I gotta say, it was unsettling."

The group quieted. They were all thinking about what Gal had just told them.

When they all looked at Tuss again, it made him uncomfortable, "Well, okay then. Here it is, I don't know how exactly I should I put it, but," he paused to gather his thoughts, "When do we begin to find meaning and purpose? We're all agreed that being dragonflies is the best thing possible. We accept that living as a community, you know, like we've been, is about the best thing ever, right?"

No one disagreed.

"So, life's good for us right now. But what else is there? I think that's what I'm trying to get at." He looked at his friends, hoping they understood. "Do any of you feel like there has to be more? And, if so, that it might involve other kinds of creatures eventually?" Tuss rose from his perch, hovered about in a circle. He called down to his somewhat confused friends. "Everywhere I turn, everyplace I look; the meadows, the Fen, the swamp and even here, as a new game of Capture is just beginning." They looked in the direction he was facing. Dozens of sleek dragonflies were organizing themselves into offensive and defensive formations.

He dropped back down and finished his thought. "Everywhere I look I see only dragonflies. They only interact with other dragonflies. I'm afraid that we're becoming the very thing that we, for lack of a better term, rebelled against."

"How's that?" Cas asked curiously.

"Yeah, who's rebelled from what?" Ace asked, sounding very confused.

"We did, all of us," answered Tuss.

Briza spoke up before Tuss had a chance to elaborate more, "I understand what he's saying now. You're right. If we keep following the exact same routine day in and day out, we'll end up just like the old order. Those boring, stodgy dragonflies that always follow the strictest interpretation of the Tradition, whether it makes sense or not."

"I understand now, but did we really rebel?"

"Yes and no, Ace," Leon answered, "We just did what we did, which isn't quite the Traditional way of the dragonfly."

"Leon's right too, but back on topic. As Tuss and Briza have said; if we continue as we've been, day after day, given enough time and repetition, we'll eventually see all ways of living aside from our own as unacceptable," Gal said.

"That makes my head hurt," Coria said.

"Mine, too," agreed Ace.

"All I'm saying is that we need to be very careful that we don't become what we've avoided so far."

"Do you think that's happening to us?" Mira asked in a quiet voice.

"Not yet Mira," Gal placed a lot of emphasis on the yet.

"Well, I'm not going to worry about it. Things are too much

fun right now," Briza said.

"I believe you when you say that, Briza. But my questions remain. What's our purpose? What are we supposed to be doing? Is what we've done so far all that there is?" Tuss waited for answers. He would be happy for just one. When none were forthcoming, he broke the broody quiet. "Are the rest of you getting as bored as I am?"

No one said a thing.

"That's it? Just silence? No answers, Briza? And the rest of you?" Tuss allowed some anger to creep into his voice. "You always have something to say and often enough, too much, but not now?" For the first time since they'd emerged, there was real friction between the friends. Tuss couldn't believe that he was in the middle of it. He couldn't believe that it was he that had started it. He seldom lost his temper, especially not over something as silly as a few unanswered questions.

"Tuss!" Cas said in a way he couldn't ignore.

He looked at her.

"Take it easy, we're just talking, okay?" She waited, watching to see how he would react. When he didn't respond, she continued, "I doubt any of us have answers to those questions."

Tuss drew in a deep breath, looked into Cas' eyes and felt himself relax. He was very glad that she interrupted when she did. "Yeah, you're right, Cas." He turned to Briza, "Sorry about that. I shouldn't have vented at you. They aren't fair questions, anyway."

"No worries Tuss, you just caught me off guard is all. Seeing you getting angry like that was something, though. If I actually had answers for you, they would have slipped right out of my mind," Briza laughed. "But, I think I've been asking myself pretty much the same things lately. Somehow though, I wasn't aware that I was doing it. That sounds crazy, doesn't it?"

"Not at all Briza. You just described what's been going on with me," Cas said.

The others chimed in then, and shared that they had similar thoughts and feelings.

"So then, where does that leave us? Any ideas?" Tuss asked.

Silence. No one wanted to speak up first, so they just perched there on the rock and looked at each other.

"Well?" Gal asked.

"I can say this much at least. I believe that when we're supposed to do something or know something or have a purpose, we'll just know it," Briza said and then waited to see what reactions he'd get. All he saw was only curiosity in his friend's eyes. "It seems to me that figuring out the way things work around the Fen, you know, things like everyday life, has been left up to us. It hardly makes sense to me, but it does feel that way, doesn't it?"

"Well that seems a bit convenient don't you think? We'll know what we're supposed to, when we're supposed to?" Cas asked.

Briza started to color.

"Hold on Cas, I think I understand what he's saying and he's right. It's not like we can just ask someone what we're supposed to do, what our purpose is. What I think he means is that we'll know because we're on our own, so in a sense, it's left up to us. He means that we've no choice but to make the best decisions we possibly can given whatever circumstance we're in," Coria said in a rush.

"Ummm, except we can ask your friend Auran," Mira added.

"Maybe, Mira. He won't always answer everything," Cas said.

"There's more to it for us, though. We have the Tradition, not the part about isolation but the rest as a guide and we do have a decent amount of experiences to fall back on. I know we aren't anything approaching old and wise or even close to knowing what someone like Auran does. But..." Briza hesitated.

"That may be about the most sensible thing you've ever said Briza,"

Gal complimented, "and I can see by the look in your eyes that you've no clue as to why I just said that, right?"

"Ouch, give me a little credit," Briza answered, "I'm not as look as I *are* obtuse!"

"Oh yes you are," Cas said. Briza responded by laughing, the others joined in, but only when they saw her teasing didn't anger him.

After their moment of fun, Cas asked, "What are the two of you saying exactly?"

"I think they're saying more or less, what I was getting at with my questions, but we haven't come to any conclusions yet. Right?" Tuss wasn't really looking for an answer this time. He knew he was simply saying what everyone was thinking.

They talked a while longer about the other creatures, both strange and normal that lived around the Fen. They talked about the possibilities that life might hold for them and about the uncertain but exciting future that stretched out before them.

After a time the conversation died out, so they just perched together in silence. The rock they were on was now completely covered in shade. The day had been warm; its bright sunlight had shone down on the spot for the entire morning, and most of the afternoon. The rocks in general were comfortable, even in the shadows; the heat stored in them radiated out slowly. Being dragonflies, they enjoyed the warmth. They needed it to live and fly. Without it, their bodies would stiffen and their wings would feel like great sluggish weights.

Tuss broke the long silence. "So, here's where we are, or where I think we are. Correct me if I'm wrong. We've more or less concluded that we all feel a need to find our purpose and that when we find it, or when it finds us we'll know because it'll make sense and we probably won't have a lot of choice in the matter?"

They agreed.

Ace spoke up hesitantly, "I think it's a lot like our emergence. It was time for that great change. Some of us didn't want it, some of us did, for me it was like dying"

"Ah, the old passes away for the new to replace it!" Mira was excited by the idea.

"Exactly! Change is like dying but some things have to die so other things can live," Ace added.

"And that new living thing, much like what we're supposed to be, that purpose Briza was going on about. That's what we'll know and I think we'll know because it will make sense and we'll grow into it or it will make us grow, willing or not," Aneth lost his train of thought.

"Okay, okay, that hurts my head. Make it stop please!" Tuss said, "but don't get me wrong, I can live with all of that for now." He sighed, half in contentment, half in impatience, knowing that there was nothing he could do to change things or stop the inevitable.

"There's also the other thing that we haven't really addressed yet. I think it's sort of the same subject too, the boredom. It can't be just me that's bored." Before anyone could get defensive, Tuss explained, "Don't get me wrong. I love the games and all, but believe it or not, I feel the need for some change in that area, and hopefully soon. Call it a short break from routine, I guess."

"Change, how?" Cas asked.

"Well for starters, I think that tomorrow, I'm going to begin exploring the lands around the Fen. I'd love to know what surrounds us here. I mean, all of this time we've spent in the east meadows, I have a feeling that whatever is out there; where we haven't been yet, at the very least, it won't be boring. Any of you interested in joining me?"

All eight said yes at exactly the same instant. That started them laughing again.

"Well, that's settled then," Tuss said with finality when the laughter quieted.

All about the meadow, the games and noise of the other dragonflies was dying down. Most of the players had flown off for the evening. There were areas to patrol and meals to be hawked. Tuss and his friends joined the exodus and flew off across the darkening fields towards the Fen. The sun was still burning brightly, turning more orange than yellow, getting lower on the horizon.

Part of its glowing immensity was hidden behind the bulk of the DragonTree. The shadowy silhouette cast across the surface of the water was impressive and frightful. The great Tree looked like it was on fire, the brilliant evening sky lighting it up from behind. The mist rising from the cooling water added to the phenomenon. It was a magnificent sight.

Tuss could nearly picture in his mind that the Tree itself was a large creature, one that was breathing fire and smoke. It made him feel strange, and he wondered again how it got its name.

"We better take care of our responsibilities before we lose more of the light," he told his companions.

The evening gloaming lasted long after the sun went down, and that was more than enough time for them to fly a patrol and hawk their fill. They finished their time together in the dark, talking until the sky was full of bright stars, knowing that once the heat from their bodies was gone, they'd have to retire to their separate perches and wait for the warmth of the morning sun.

Then they could embark upon their adventures.

"LOOK!" shouted Ace.

The rest looked sleepily her way. Mira started to protest the disruption of the peace until she like the rest, followed the tilt of Ace's head. What they saw amazed them.

Bright streaks blazed through the night sky far overhead. One after another, they started as a point of light in the north and then grew into flashing, pulsing ribbons of cold fire, trailing sparks as they passed over the Fen and burned towards the southern horizon. The companions eyes were dazzled repeatedly until whatever the mysterious objects were, disappeared.

Everything around them seemed blacker than ever.

It happened again. The night sky lit up and silhouetted the mountainous crags lining the southern horizon, making them look like jagged bat teeth.

"What is it?" Mira shrieked.

"I've no idea but it's beautiful," Cas replied breathlessly.

The others, even Briza at least for the moment, were hushed with awe.

The strange light show continued. It was similar to the lightning that came to the Fen but without the booming thunder. The sound that accompanied this phenomena was a sort of buzzing or sizzle.

"It's like the sky itself is on fire!" Ace said nervously.

Tuss thought, *all that light, the burning and diffusion of sparks. It's like nothing from this world.*

"I think the stars are falling," Briza suggested, once he had enough self control to speak.

His words gave Tuss a start, *wasn't that more or less what occurred to me?*

"Oh sure Briza, you must've shaken them loose with your amazing game playing abilities today. It just took until now for them to reach us," Leon laughed.

Briza didn't react.

"Whatever it is, it's about over," Aneth said.

One last *star* rushed overhead. The rippling Fen reflected its flashing brilliance many times over. The reeds the friends perched on danced with complex patterns of light. They would remember this spectacular moment of celestial wonder for the rest of their lives.

Chapter Eight

We Were Wrong

Tuss awoke to the sound of raised voices. He recognized a couple, they sounded angry, very angry. Briza's was one, which wasn't a big surprise. Tuss had heard his friend's voice raised in anger on many occasions. The true surprise came with hearing one of the others; it was Coria's and he'd never once heard her sound anything like she did now.

Uhoh! This can't be good, Tuss sighed deeply, his heart sinking. *Did it have to happen, whatever it was, on today of all days? The day when we're planning to start exploring. Oh well!* He was about to go and see what all the excitement was about, when he realized that he was having a hard time stretching his wings. He knew right then that he'd made a mistake. He didn't remember to perch on the morning sun side of the reeds. The night had been chilly, too. So without the heat of the direct sunlight, he was stiff. He could fly but it would be uncomfortable and awkward until his body warmed.

He leapt from the reed, groaning and telling himself again, *remember, perch in a better spot tonight, one that gets the first sunlight.*

He beat at the air, rising above the Fen's surface, whirled around and headed in the direction of the noisy voices.

Briza was hardly pausing for breath, his ranting and raving, which, loud before, grew in volume still.

Oh wow! Someone or something must have made him really angry.

Ignoring his stiffness, Tuss hurried towards the disturbance. He wanted to see what was up and quickly. As he neared the source of noise and trouble, he could see the shapes of dozens, hovering on the periphery. All of them were watching the same thing, Briza, Coria and several older dragonflies. They spread about in a loose circle, facing inwards and looking extremely upset.

Friends, he thought, *I love them, but sometimes...*

Briza and Coria weren't alone. They were surrounded by several of the young dragonflies that played Capture.

One of the *newcomers* as Tuss thought of the four, was an intimidating Comet Darner. He was huge, his flaming red abdomen was thick and long and looked very menacing. He was easily three times Briza's or Coria's size. He also looked like he was ready for combat, the territorial kind. The whole tableau was a frightening sight to see, one that Tuss knew he'd never forget; his two small friends hovering eye to eye with a monster of a dragonfly. And what was even more impressive, they weren't just facing that huge Darner, the three Elders of DragonTree were there too. Tuss felt his initial frustration wane as pride of friendship swelled within. His two small friends looked unafraid, even facing impossible odds.

Wow! Just wow! Look at them!

Worry about actual violence faded when he reminded himself that these days, when dragonflies of the Fen had confrontations, it was ritualistic and seldom ended in physical hurt. His kind had altered their habits long ago. The histories were full of terrible tales of challenges that went too far. Tuss tried to recall the story about Platanus, there was a specific detail about him and how he helped to change the way their kind lived and interacted, but it was a bit fuzzy. He'd have to ask Cas if she remembered anything about it, later.

He moved a little closer so he could hear more clearly what was being said.

105

"You! You come around here now and after all this time? After we've been on our own, figuring everything out for ourselves. And now this *meeting*, all of a sudden, you want to tell us what's right and wrong about how we've done things, and worst of all, what we should do from now on? Just like that? You actually expect us to listen? Are you kidding me?" Briza was barely keeping his temper. His entire body from eyes to claspers was trembling with the effort to maintain what little control he did have.

The Elders didn't answer. They just hovered, apparently confused by the confrontation. The big red Darner's body, much like Briza's, was almost shaking with tension.

But he doesn't look any more imposing than my smaller friend. Interesting, thought Tuss.

"Tradition you say? We need to stop our foolishness and start living by the old-style, DragonTree Tradition? Right here, right now?" Briza's anger filled voice also had a hint of chagrin coloring it. "Weeks go by and everything's fine, we hear nothing from any of you aside from that one brief visit. And now you show up here, IN MY SECTION OF THE FEN, UNINVITED, to tell me, no! To tell us, that we need to adjust our behavior and live by *'Our kind's Traditions'*. I'm sorry but that's just lunacy!"

"It sure is. I couldn't have said it better, Briza," Coria's high-pitched voice spat out the words as she looked at the Elders. There wasn't a hint of fear in her eyes, nor in her bearing. She let her voice drop to a more normal, conversational level and added, "and just so you know, Briza speaks for all of us, you'd better listen to him."

She spun in a circle indicating the young dragonflies surrounding them, they numbered close to a hundred now. With each passing exchange in the confrontation, many more were arriving, singularly and in groups. Apparently, all the nearby folk of the Fen wanted to see what all of the hubbub was about.

"Young one," the female Elder said in a kind voice, "we're not here to tell any of you how to live. We're merely suggesting that you recall the training and the teaching you had before your emergence. How did you put it, *'just weeks ago'*, wasn't it?" She paused waiting for an answer. Coria said nothing. "You couldn't have forgotten what you were taught, not so soon." Her voice was soothing, under control and Tuss respected her for it. He wouldn't have guessed that anyone, let alone an Elder, would have so much reserve and calm under the circumstances. He'd experienced what it was like to face Briza when he was at his worst which was a trying situation at best. And it wasn't just Briza the kindly Elder was dealing with.

"Suggesting?" Briza sputtered.

"Yes, we suggest only," one of the male Elders said gently.

He was very old, so old in fact that he'd lost most of his coloring; his scarred body a mixture of washed out grays. Whatever color he'd been when he was fresh from the underwater world was long gone. He did, however, still have jet black bands forming ringlets around his abdomen, from eyes to claspers, and they looked healthy and shiny. His wings were cloudy and all four had tattered edges. One was very rough along the leading edge. The old flier had obviously lived a long and active life. Looking at this Elder made Tuss feel very young.

How are Briza and Coria able to hover before them like that? There's something noble and awe inspiring about them... The audacity of his two friends impressed Tuss, yet one more time.

Briza's voice broke into his thought process.

"I'm not so young or unthinking that I don't know what I've just been told. I mean no disrespect, but I assure you that what I heard a moment ago from him," Briza looked at the third Elder, the youngest of the three, "was not a suggestion, it was a command, actually it was several of them." He paused, almost as if he was expecting to be rebuked. When it didn't come, he went on. "He didn't just *suggest* either, he came here and told us that we needed to stay put in our individual sections. He told us that we should *'immediately curtail all of our other inappropriate activities'*." Briza said the last bit in a dry, derisive voice, obviously trying to imitate the younger Elder. He was still addressing the older two directly, while referring to the one whom he'd just mocked.

Tuss couldn't help but notice that this younger Elder looked a lot like he and Cas, just a little bigger and much darker. He was a Blue Dasher too, but mature enough to have the deeper shade of coloring, common in adults of their specific kind. Tuss also noticed that Briza was responding to the serene tones of the two senior Elders. He was calming himself down by degrees. It was visible in his coloration, the whirl of his eyes and his posture. Tuss was happy to see his friend adapt to the situation. When others were calm Briza was able to respond in kind. It was even more proof that his friend was growing up and maturing. *One day he may even become a respectable dragonfly.* Tuss laughed quietly to himself. He would have to share his last thought with all of the friends, just to see what Briza's reaction might be. Would the maturing process still be at work a day from now, two days, a week? He and his friends were growing up in so many ways. Each new day seemed to offer some new evidence that proved that fact.

The younger male Elder finally spoke, "Little one," he said in a smug voice. He paused allowing his insulting tone to have its desired effect.

Calling Briza *little one* was very rude and obviously meant to unsettle the upstart. It worked. Briza tensed again, his calm was gone in a flash. This Elder was obviously much less willing to show the young dragonflies the same respect his two seniors had.

"You called me little one?" Briza kept his voice steady. In fact, it was calm and flat, without any of the typical anger such a thing would normally have stirred.

Uh-oh! That's not good, not good at all, thought Tuss. Briza sounded dangerous, ready to engage. Tuss wondered if it was time for him to interrupt.

"That's correct, little one. I don't plan to argue with you any longer. Our Tradition is simple and clear. You must abide by it. You're a dragonfly and it's our way. It's your way too, like it or not." The rude Elder raised his voice to address the rest of crowd. "All of you must abide by the Tradition as well; how else may we maintain our community? Hasn't it been this way for years beyond memory? Why would anyone desire to have it otherwise? Our Tradition works. I've lived long by it. My two fellow Elders, Rumex and Gnaphalium have lived even longer thus. It's served us well enough."

The other two said nothing. They just hovered there, neither agreeing nor disagreeing. Murmurs of both dissent and agreement could be heard as they were being passed back and forth amongst the observers. Several arguments broke out.

"That's strange," Cas whispered to Tuss. "The way the two aged Elders said nothing just then." He was so surprised by the sound of her voice coming from right beside him, he all but fell out of the air. She laughed while he did his best to recover quickly and hide his embarrassment.

He knew he wasn't fooling her, but he still tried to sound casual as he replied, "It sure is. They didn't respond, did they?" Tuss answered.

"They sure didn't," Aneth affirmed. He'd flown over too. Tuss berated himself for missing their arrival and for not paying proper attention to his surroundings.

Briza, even as furious as he was, now faced with such opposition began to waver. He must have somehow missed the significance of the non-response of the other two Elders. His entire bearing began to change, his body started to sag with defeat.

"Ahhh, good. I see that you're hearing the sense of our words. Give it some time," the younger Elder said, his tone more smug than ever. Tuss wanted to fly over to the obnoxious fool and knock him about.

Aneth must have too. His voice rumbled deeply with anger. "Enough is enough!"

Gal and Leon, who'd joined them, were feeling the same way. All four of the riled males began to move. If it weren't for Cas hissing at them to stay put, all of them might have done something they'd be sorry for later.

"Give it enough time and all of you will understand that our ways work best. You'll learn to appreciate the peace and quiet. You'll find that independence and solitude go well together and satisfy the heart and mind much more than the noisy activity you seem so fond of."

Aneth moved forward again. Cas moved too, placing herself between Aneth and the object of his growing wrath. Tuss didn't know what to do. He was torn between flying over there and tearing the wings off the smug fool or doing what Briza was doing, giving in. He was at an impasse. Before, it seemed like two of the Elders were being reasonable. They were at the very least showing much more respect than the obnoxious one was.

There was a long silence where no one moved, nothing was being said.

"No!" stated Coria, clear and strong.

Tuss remembered just then the name of the younger Elder. It was Salix, and he reacted in astonishment to Coria's one word proclamation. The look in his eyes was a mix of confusion and shock. He must have thought that he had the situation under control.

"Excuse me, what was that little one? It was you that spoke, correct?" he asked even as he hovered nearer to her either trying to threaten or intimidate. *Is he trying to impress her with his larger size?* Tuss wondered. *He sure doesn't know what he's getting himself into!* For whatever reason the blatant act broke all of the tension he was feeling up to that point. Tuss began to laugh quietly. Cas joined him; soon enough the others did, too. They could see that Coria was in a state she only attained while in the midst of battle. It was her Capture-mode they were witnessing. They knew personally just how frightening a creature she could become when aroused like she was. They waited anxiously for what was to come next.

"Yes, it was me that spoke and I said No! And I say it again, No!" Coria stated with authority. Beside her, Briza was regaining his confidence. Coria's timely participation was all he'd needed.

"Huh?" was all that Salix could mutter.

Tuss couldn't believe it. He whispered to Cas, "I knew she had it in her, but to actually witness this!"

Cas shushed him.

"No! No and no! Is that clear enough for you?" Coria's wings trembled with anger.

Tuss forced himself to look away from the Elder, Salix. He didn't want to start laughing out loud. The sight of his friend, a small, bright red dragonfly facing him down was too much. He saw that Rumex and Gnaphalium had bright swirling eyes. His heart leapt within him, it may have even skipped a beat or two. *Is it possible that those two really aren't going to be as unreasonable as Salix?* He looked back at Coria. She was speaking again.

"You can't tell us how to live," she paused to allow her words to have time to sink in and then went on, "We don't have to listen. You're certainly welcome to suggest and demand all you want, but that's where it all ends!"

She was like a force of nature. Tuss loved watching her, such a fierce and beautiful creature, and a miniature storm unto herself. She spoke in a way that increased her stature tenfold and gave the impression that she was full of wrath and fury, a dragonfly not to be trifled with.

"I'm glad it's not me she's talking to like that," Aneth said with respect.

"No kidding," Leon said.

"Yeah," agreed Cas, "She's something else!"

"Shhh, he's about to get himself in deeper," Ace quieted them.

"And how's that, little one? I'm an Elder, elected and appointed, holder of the position for many years. How do you tell me no, when I've had our Tradition to rely upon as my guide. Not to mention the authority of my office?" It was clear that Salix wasn't about to back down.

"Easily," Coria said casually.

Tuss couldn't stifle his laughter anymore. The scene was just too humorous. He tried hard to stay as quiet as possible, but when he heard others all around him beginning to laugh out loud he quit holding his laughter back.

Salix looked angrily about himself. He clearly wanted to say something to those that found the situation so funny, but Coria wasn't finished.

"I say no because of the Tradition, not in spite of the Tradition. By the Tradition, you say that we're to be independent. I say okay to that. And further, I understand that point to mean that I live on my own. I'm to support the community by taking my independent responsibilities to DragonTree and the Fen seriously. That's accomplished by the proper stewardship of my section of the Fen, patrolling, hawking and so forth." She was quoting almost word for word from some of the teachings they'd had as young students. "And when I accomplish that stewardship, that's it. There's nothing beyond that, as far as I've been taught, that you or anyone else can hold me accountable for. Not in light of the whole independence issue. Is there something I missed?"

She had everyone's attention now, laughing or not.

Tuss thought that if she was made aware of the number of witnesses to her tirade or better put, speech, she'd become very self conscious. This wasn't everyday behavior for Coria. At least not outside of the world of the games they played.

"No, little one, you did not miss anything. You did, however, reinforce my points. Though you did so with a disturbing amount of impertinence, which shows a lack of proper respect for..."

Coria cut him off by turning about in midair. She began to fly away. Tuss felt immediate disappointment. *Was she giving up?*

As the smug look began to return to Salix' eyes, Coria stopped, turned back around to face Salix and steadied herself for one last point.

"Okay then, it's respect you want? Have it your way. I'll show you the respect that you're demanding, but in turn, I demand the same from you. You know what I'm talking about, the kind of respect due me as a member of the DragonTree community."

Tuss wanted to cheer. Some of the others actually did.

"How's that?" Salix asked. He sounded a little less confident now.

"By Tradition is how! What else?" she said.

Salix said nothing.

"Yes! By Tradition. See now," she looked up at the rising sun, "it's past time for me to be on my way. I've my patrols to do and you've made me late. I desire to go hawking, because I'm hungry and I'll do both in my section of the Fen as Tradition dictates." She paused, glaring at him for emphasis, daring him to interrupt her. "Once I'm full and contented that my section of the Fen is secure, my responsibilities accomplished, all by Tradition, I'll go and do as I see fit with the rest of my day. I'll accomplish this too, according to my Tradition of independence. I'll do it all, as you've said, by Tradition and by Tradition I fully expect, NO! I demand that you leave me be and allow me the freedom and respect of my independence, meaning, LEAVE ME ALONE!" She shouted the last part so everyone all over the Fen could hear it. Then, in her more usual, sweet voice, "By Tradition, spoken before the other two more reasonable Elders, my friends and my neighbors, I demand it again. And with all due respect, I ask you to leave my area of Fen. We've been drifting a bit in the morning breeze, the result being that you are now a trespasser in my area. Please remove yourself promptly or face a physical challenge. Thank you!"

Salix was speechless, in shock, and it was a sight for all to see.

"Oh and one last thing," she continued in her sweet voice. "You've called me *little one* more than once. I noticed that you called my friend the same. I think you even referred to most of those here as *little ones* at some point or another in this conversation." She waited a beat, allowing him to respond. He didn't have anything to say. "Doing so was very disrespectful, but we can forgive that, can't we?" she asked as she turned to face the very large crowd gathered about her. She didn't wait for an answer and turned back to Salix. "You see, I know that when you call me *little one* you're just being ill-mannered, trying to put me in my place. You're demeaning me personally and at the same time you're diminishing the position you hold. Your treatment of me so far has been well below that which I'd expect from an Elder, that is, if what I was taught about the Elders of the past is true."

She sighed deeply, it was an old and tired sound. "I offer my apologies to Rumex and Gnaphalium and I hope I've not shown either of you any discourtesy. In time, I'll probably apologize to you, Salix, if I conclude that I was out of line. Thank you, good hawking and a bright, warm day to all of you." She flew off to the sound of cheers. It wasn't only the young dragonflies cheering, either. It was coming from everyone but Salix. He was smiling though, and that was a marvel. Tuss wondered if Coria had affected him somehow. It didn't make sense, but he couldn't deny it. The youngest Elder was smiling and it looked genuine.

"Wow! She must've touched him deeply or won him over or something," Cas said happily. "I would've expected the worst possible reaction from that stubborn old dragonfly. Maybe, just maybe, Coria and Briza have done all of us a huge favor. What do you think?"

"I think you're correct and on top of that, I can't wait to let them know how proud I am of them," answered Tuss.

"Well then, what are we waiting for? Let's go tell them!" Ace said.

"Did you see the other two Elders? They acted like they approved of the way things went," Gal said. "I wouldn't believe it was possible if someone told me, but having witnessed it. I'm almost dumbfounded."

"Gal, there's nothing dumb about you my friend, nothing at all," Tuss said.

Gal just laughed in response.

Off the seven of them flew, wanting first to congratulate their friends and then to get started on their morning routines and responsibilities. For all but Tuss, the plans for exploration were momentarily forgotten. He decided not to remind them, the timing was wrong now and he'd decided that he wanted to chat with Auran first. Another day or two of gaming wouldn't hurt them. There was no rush, they were young and the world wasn't going anywhere. Their adult lives would last much longer than when they were nymphs. *And anyway, I'm so full of energy after witnessing all of that. I need to burn it off in the east meadows. I think I've come up with a new strategy too.*

Chapter Nine

The Games

Tuss looked out from the shaded cover of a large bush. What he saw was the bright, hazy sunlit fields and meadows that lay just beyond the edge of the great eastern woods. Leon, Mira and Ace were beside him, ready to spring into flight. They were only waiting for his command, once given they'd break from cover and speed towards the boulder that jutted up from the surrounding brush. The objective in this game of Capture was a prominent outcropping, bare, rounded and exposed. The idea was to have one of their teammates perch upon it and hold position untagged for the time it took to fly across the Fen.

They were playing as far from home as they dared. The east edge of the grassland that defined the gaming field was bordered by a copse of trees and brush too tangled for even the smallest of them to comfortably fly through. In their experience, places dark and mysterious were best avoided, they were residence to spiders and possibly worse. There was however a long and narrow meadow, which separated the northern and southern arms of the forest that ran from where they played to unexplored lands beyond. As far as any of them knew, this small break was the only open access connecting the Fen region and what lay east. Once, Tuss had flown to the far end to see what he could. The lands were wild and strange. The lush grassland meadows he was used to gave way to scrub and vast stretches of ugly, thorny vegetation and on the far horizon, a mysterious forest.

Tuss wanted to play a match or two in that narrow section of meadow when the time was right. The thick trees on both sides would act as boundaries making it the perfect spot to learn close quarters combat. Gaming there would be something new for everyone and offered interesting possibilities.

When they finished the day's events, he'd ask Briza, Gal and Aneth what they thought about the idea. He already knew that Cas would have a lot to add; she was turning into a master strategist. She'd been the one to put the idea into his head to begin with. *Hmmm,* he thought, *I may as well just ask her instead of the other three. She's more likely than not to have thought it all the way through. She probably has some clever plan devised already.*

His Wing was the bait today. They were supposed to draw the defenders out and away from the boulder. If they timed it right and successfully followed the plan, a win was assured. Aneth, Briza, Cas and Gal would mimic Tuss' Wing, only from a different direction. Both groups would be flying as fast as they could, shouting the entire time, making as much a spectacle of themselves as possible. The key was to pull the defenders away from the *base* where the objective was and trick them into chasing decoys.

Thymus and his Wing of smaller, faster fliers were waiting in the treetops; they would try and counter the defenders when and if they responded. They would abandon their cover, drop down from on high, flying in with the sun behind them and add to the havoc Tuss' and Aneth's Wings had hopefully set into motion.

The action plan was a good one. In the pre-game strategy session, everyone was invited to contribute ideas. This large, complex and carefully timed assault was the most audacious idea they'd ever attempted. Aneth had stated that, "the games are getting larger and more complex, therefore the strategies should follow suit." So here they were, split into four Wings, with no means of communicating. Their chance for victory came down to good timing, intuition, mutual trust and days upon days' worth of past cooperation.

They were playing against a very good team, but Tuss knew that his team, The League, was better. They worked well together; were cohesive and flexible. If improvisation were necessary, they'd adapt on the fly and respond as required. Everyone had a role to play, knowing that each member doing their part was integral to success. They took their responsibilities to the group seriously.

Teamwork, thought Tuss, *that's what sets us apart. We're better as a group than we are as individuals. We've learned to take advantage of Aneth, Leon and Gals' larger size just as we use the smaller speedier Coria, Briza, Acer and Mira for quick attacks and Thymus' Wing of skilled, diverse fliers could play any role. Hmmm, I guess that leaves Cas and I to sort of float between responsibilities. That's interesting. We need to figure out how the two of us can be better used.*

Teamwork, they'd learned that ultimate principal long ago, during the first week of games. It'd carried them from one win to another; their record, though no one but Briza was actually keeping track, was perfect. The other teams suffered from the same basic fault, they played as individuals, each doing their own thing. In other words, as typical dragonflies, slaves to their nature.

Not us though! Not ever. We've learned that much at least. Our nature has as good a side as it does a bad. Tuss felt excitement burst within. He loved being part of something larger than himself, becoming something better by refusing to be self-serving. Others mattered, and the more he focused on their wants and needs rather than his own, the happier he'd become.

With that in mind, he and Cas had recruited Thymus and several of his friends to join their League. Together, the two groups, once they learned to know and trust each other, were unbeatable. The day was coming when they'd have to break into two teams. It'd be necessary for the sake of change and growth but that meant they'd eventually play against each other. *One of us will lose for the first time. I'm not looking forward to that and then again I am. It'll certainly be very interesting.*

Of all the other dragonflies the nine had met since emergence, Thymus was the most like them. They were surprised to find that they also had very similar ideas about life around the Fen.

Thymus turned out to be a good leader once he was given the opportunity to prove himself. As Tradition required, he'd removed himself from his emergence friends, moving into a quiet, lonely existence. The games were his personal catalyst for change. Because of them, Thymus and those he winged around with were finding more joy and freedom than they'd previously known. The bond that'd formed between the two groups had forged them into one. It was the sort of relationship that would last forever and allow them to grow in skill and friendship. The effect the nine, kind-of-sort-of, innocently rebellious dragonflies had on others spread to every corner of the Fen, much like ripples spreading across the water.

So yeah, at least for today, thought Tuss, *the outcome is predictable. We'll win this one easily enough.* He knew the opposition would fall for the deception. They wouldn't work together, none of the other teams had yet learned the patience that good teamwork required. They'd be lured out of their strong position by both groups of decoys. He doubted that a single one of the defenders would bother to remain behind and protect the objective. And even if they do leave one or two behind, Thymus will adjust quickly, split his Wing in two and roll up whoever is left.

The League was a force to be reckoned with. Coria would undoubtedly be the one to sneak in unnoticed, untouched and finish the match.

"Tuss!" Ace hissed at him, shaking him from his thoughts.

Oops! I better put my mind back in the game or I'll not hear the end of it. "Yeah sorry. I got a little lost there!"

"You sure did! Well?"

It was time. Ace may as well have been leading. She was the one paying attention.

"NOW!" Tuss shouted.

His Wing flew from the shadows and into the sunlight. The sound of his voice hadn't finished echoing through the trees before they were fully involved.

Oh! He thought as he leapt away from his perch, *if we delayed longer, we would've stiffened in the cooling shade. That's my bad!*

In a few quick wing-beats they were up to full speed. They were fast but the opponents were equally so and responded immediately. He was impressed. They were quick and ready. He wondered if the carefully arranged plan might actually fail. The defenders for all accounts looked like they'd planned something of their own.

"See that?" asked Ace as she raced towards the oncoming players. A patrol sweeping a guarding pattern around the objective was responding too.

"Yeah, nothing we can do about it, we're in until everything plays out!" he answered.

"How'd we miss it?"

"We're getting lazy and presumptive and they're learning fast."

Ace laughed, "It will make this match more challenging."

"Uh-huh. But I hate when my mistakes get our side tagged!"

"Oh well, it's just a game."

He wasn't so sure about her last statement. He could hear the shouted *war cries* as they flew and became engaged. Briza had been the first of them to give voice to his excitement when the thrill of play took hold in those early days of play. Then it was Coria and soon after that, it was everyone.

There's nothing else like it, hearing dozens of happy dragonflies shouting their exuberant cries as they flew into battle. Tuss added his own shout to the loud, fierce chorus and it was exhilarating. He was flying as fast as he was able, being chased by the defenders drawn from their positions. He loved hearing the rushing noise of the wind, the whirring of wings, the players and the general chaos erupting all around him.

This is good, really good. Life at its best. I'm flying, really flying!

The attack was in full swing; there was no stopping what they'd begun. Once set in motion, speed and distance made it impossible to plan further. Improvisation would be key.

Tuss could see bright flashes of color blazing in towards the center of the opponent's base. They zipped all about in crazy, erratic patterns, shouting and laughing the entire time. The defenders were splitting into pairs breaking away from the larger group. *That's not a bad move.* He knew that pairing off was a very good defensive strategy, one that demonstrated forethought and self-control. *It won't help them today though, they've taken the bait and fallen for the trick.* Leaving only two players behind to defend was a mistake and they'd pay for it. *They'll learn something new today and will adjust before the next game.*

The League's attackers broke off, just as planned. They turned about, mere wing-beats from the objective, aiming themselves in every other direction. The defenders gave chase in their pairs and the real battle was finally begun. The players from both sides zoomed about in a winged frenzy. Shouts, taunts and laughter erupted even louder. This sort of action was fun for everyone. Bedlam reigned. They were born for this. They were flying, they were in action. They were dragonflies.

Onlookers not of dragonfly-kind would think that the group of them had gone stark raving mad. Most would also assume that the crazy creatures were trying to hurt one another. Both assumptions would be absolutely incorrect, but seeing a mass of them swarming all about in the bright sunlight, making such a cacophonous noise could also put fear into the heart of any observer. The players themselves knew differently, everything made sense. The ebb and flow of the game, created for them a beautiful, perfect rhythm that filled their lives with joy.

High above the tumult Thymus saw what he was waiting for. He called out loudly, his Wing answering him. Tuss heard the shouts as the only unengaged element of the League began their attack, swooping straight in towards the center of the brightly colored storm that'd enveloped the meadow.

Now, if everyone sticks to the plan we'll win, my mistake aside. Tuss' only remaining worry as always was whether their nature would prevail over careful planning. None of them could predict just how long dragonflies could be counted on to cooperate together.

But this feels right. To be here doing this. I wonder if the others would agree? He remembered the last time he was distracted like this during a game, he'd removed himself from the action. Tuss felt the same now as he did then. There was more to it this time; he almost felt like they were not playing so much as they were training for something. *That's an interesting twist, I wonder if it means anything?*

Shouting and laughing interrupted. He snapped his thoughts back to the present. He knew that Coria must have started her run by now. She would have been further back in the shadows than any of them, waiting for the right moment. Once she saw Thymus and his Wing come down from the treetops she'd go, no need to command her. She knew what to do and when. Coria was the best of them at Capture.

Tuss slowed down and hovered. It was time to watch the plan play out. He was so far from the center of action, his presence or lack thereof wouldn't make a difference. He didn't even mind the rough tags he felt brush the top of his thorax; he knew it was coming. It was two defenders, one closely followed by another. They were doing their part for their team.

He cried, "I'm out!" loud enough for anyone nearby to hear. Two tags were enough. Tuss was considered a great prize when, and if, he was tagged. A fortunate opponent would brag for days if they were the one that got Tussilago, leader of The League.

The two dragonflies that'd tagged him looked confused but happy. First he'd led them all about in a mad chase, easily avoiding contact, and then he'd just stopped, making it all too easy on them. Did he give himself up?

"What gives, Tuss?" one of the two defenders asked.

"I'll tell you what gives. Your defenses, that's what gives. Look what's happened to it! There's only a few of you left." His voice was filled with pride.

Tuss laughed hard as the two sped off in a vain attempt to try and stop the inevitable. The match was already over, their efforts would be wasted, though well intentioned. Aneth, Briza, Thymus, Mira, Gal and the rest of The League had the clear advantage. Numbers didn't lie; their side had more players remaining. The defenders could only delay the inevitable.

The two that had tagged Tuss joined their teammates in the last desperate stand, only to be eliminated by the much faster Briza. He got both as he made a twisting dive straight between them, one right after the other, voicing a wild cry as he did so. His whole personality changed while playing; he was like someone or something else entirely. It was a bit worrisome. Tuss wondered what would happen if Briza ever did find himself in a genuine life or death struggle, he shuddered hoping he never had to witness something like that.

The Leagues' Wings had performed perfectly. There were only a few opponents remaining. One was flying crazily about, trying to get away from Briza as he shouted madly, scaring the poor young dragonfly half out of his wits. The rest still in the game were scattered so far away from the center of things, they might as well have been assigned to guard the DragonTree standing far off across field and Fen.

Spreading the defenders out was just one of the strategies that Tuss had relied upon. It'd gone flawlessly. He looked towards the base. Coria was there perched on the objective. She was sunning herself in the bright light, calmly resting on the warm stone, looking both coy and relaxed. She might be partially disappointed, since the win was far too easy. She preferred a challenge. Maybe next time he'd send her in as a decoy and have one of the others try for the capture. It wouldn't hurt to shake things up a little. Learning each other's roles would help everyone improve and keep things fresh. Unpredictability would enhance the League's winning ways. He wanted them to be a moving target of sorts, keeping the enemy off balance. There were many strategies to try, and they certainly had the time.

He sighed, "Every day is pretty much the same as the last and I forgot about meeting Auran and I forgot about exploring."

"Yeah, me too," said Cas.

Tuss jerked around, startled by her voice.

"You did it again!" he said, heart pounding.

"I did?" she said teasing him, "What exactly did I do?"

"Oh, never mind," he replied, "You heard that, huh?"

"I did."

"And?" he asked.

"And, I said, *'me too'*, as in, I agree. We should go and see Auran and we should figure out where we want to go and when to start."

Coria Captures

"Okay then," Tuss said, pleased. "That's just what we'll do."

"BREAK! BREAK!" The lone shout echoed across the meadow but was quickly picked up and chorused by many others.

Tuss and Cas were startled into action. They didn't waste time trying to locate the danger; it always came from above. The excited squawking gave the foolish birds away time and again, but having the lookouts added a more comfortable margin for escape.

The two angled straight down, flying for the dense cover the meadow's thick vegetation so generously offered.

"I hope everyone makes it this time."

"Me too!" Cas said.

A few of the younger and newer participants in recent games had been lost to the murderous birds. They either didn't know about the warnings or more likely they hadn't paid attention when the cries were called.

"But of course there's always some that think they have something to prove." Tuss sighed with relief when they reached safety. "What a horrible, senseless waste, trying to impress your friends and for what end? Becoming a bird's next meal?"

An all too familiar sound interrupted him. They both listened.

"Is that laughter I hear?" Cas asked.

"That fool!"

Briza streaked overhead followed closely by a flock of feathered monsters. He laughed, they squawked and all Cas and Tuss could do was look at each other with dismay. They'd be trapped where they were until their foolish friend tired of his antics.

"You know, he may be half the reason the others got themselves," she stopped herself. "Never mind. I'm too angry to follow that line of reasoning."

More birds arrived and either joined in the pursuit or circled above.

Everyone would just have to wait until Briza came to his senses and stopped the ridiculous sport of taunting the deadly predators.

Tuss sighed again. He heard Cas mumbling something that he couldn't quite make out. He was sure it was horrible, involved Briza's demise and was glad he'd missed most of it.

Chapter Ten

Changes Coming On

"Nope!" said Tuss. "I'd rather meet with him alone. There'll be fewer distractions that way. This is your mess, Briza. You can go and see how it plays out and then tell me about it later. I have one request, though."

"What's that, Tuss?" asked Gal.

"Please come back the way you're leaving, you know, as friends. That's all I ask, do it for me please? Would you?"

"We will, as long as the females are able to deal with having their wings handed to them," Briza said.

"WHAT!"

"HUH!"

"YEAH, RIGHT!"

"WHY, YOU..."

Cas, Mira, Ace and Coria all responded at the exact same moment, ready and willing to take Briza to task, then and there.

And there he goes again! Tuss thought.

"Joking, I'm just joking. Lighten up, would you?" Briza must have realized the trouble he'd just gotten himself into. "I wouldn't be a bit surprised if I'm the one that has to eat my words. I'm a fool, no doubt about it, but not completely. I know how good you fly, and I'm beginning to believe that you four are planning something devious. I can sense it."

"Just you wait!" Mira said confidently.

128

"I almost wish I could wait. I'm starting to doubt the wisdom of goading the four of you into this," Briza answered.

"Want to call it off, then?" asked Cas. She was giving him an easy out, one she knew he wouldn't take.

"No way! I'm not that worried. Not enough to admit defeat before I'm beaten. I just hope we can do as Tuss has asked, regardless of the outcome. That sound good?" The question surprised them. Briza didn't usually concern himself with ridiculous things like keeping the peace or getting along with others.

"Okay, but who just took over your mouth and spoke reasonable words?" Coria finally said, as the group of them readied to fly eastward together.

"Good!" Tuss said, closing off further discussion. "It sounds like you have the right idea. Have fun. I'll see you later and fill you in on what I find out." Tuss watched as his friends flew off to the meadows. With their leaving, the northern Fen quieted and he actually enjoyed the solitude for once. It was seldom that he had a moment alone during the daylight hours.

It seemed to him that all of them both dreaded and looked forward to the game they were about to play. Males versus females; it was a first, and he knew that the results would be very interesting. Everyone, including the unusually nervous Briza, had offered to go along with Tuss to meet with Auran. He told them repeatedly, 'there's no need'.

Tuss wasn't going to make today's events easier on any of them, especially Briza. The miscreant had gotten himself into the males versus females mess and he could deal with whatever came of it. It was Tuss' opinion that the males would be beaten soundly. Matched up, player to player, the females were smaller, faster and more maneuverable. It was a bad idea to begin with, but Briza wouldn't let it go once it'd entered his mind.

Maybe he'll learn to think through things a little more before opening his mouth in the future.

Flying southwest in silence, he was able to take notice of the world spread out all around him. He was reminded of the first day after emergence. The air was hot and dry and carried a strange quality. He was reminded of the sun-baked outcroppings of stones in the eastern meadows, especially when there hadn't been rain for several days. He looked south, far across the Fen, where the breeze had originated. He could see the scrubby brush and open fields that spread down from the water's edge. In the distance, rocky crags towered into the sky. None of the older dragonflies he'd spoken to could tell him anything about those jagged heights. No current resident of the Fen had traveled that far. It was strange, the whole idea of exploring beyond certain borders was never considered, it wasn't the dragonfly way. He'd heard a few tales and vague rumors about the south. More than likely, all of them fabricated by the Teachers, stories to keep the unruly in line. This only piqued Tuss' curiosity.

South, he thought, *we'll have to go south on one of our trips. It's as good a direction as any, I suppose. The feel of the breeze blowing in from those far off peaks, is very interesting!*

He felt small all of sudden, he'd seen so little. He sensed that the world was huge beyond his ability to conceive. Flying opened possibilities though, with wings, everything was a little more within his reach. *I surely won't see the whole world, it's just too big. But I'll try and see as much as I can before I die, which I hope is a long way off.*

"Enough of that!" he spoke aloud, freeing his mind from morbid thoughts. The future was a mystery, worrying about tomorrow was a waste of his time. He'd rather focus on the lovely sunny day he currently inhabited.

With mind cleared, he entered Auran's area. The sun's rays painted the looming Tree from top to bottom in a yellowish-green glow. As usual, it was an impressive sight, one that always caught him off guard. Nothing else compared, once seen it could not be forgotten. Its unique shape was a landmark that couldn't be mistaken for anything else. Tuss hovered near the reeds that grew along the bank. Auran must be off patrolling somewhere, which was odd behavior for this time of day. There was no reason for patrolling once the sun was fully risen.

Dragonflies spent the early morning and late afternoons patrolling, looking for any pests that encroached. Some they avoided, others like the frogs they ignored and endured, the rest were relegated to circumstantial need. The Fen was more or less dragonfly territory during the daytime. Once night fell however, other creatures, those that lived nocturnal lives, reigned. There was an odd assortment that called the Fen home at night and excepting the bats, most of them were reasonably friendly. Contact between the diurnal and nocturnal species was rare and almost never confrontational. The Fen was a region of peace and had been for too many years to count. Old animosities and territorial disputes were settled long ago and none still living could remember exactly who was fighting with whom and for what reasons, predators aside. The Tradition had a lot to do with it, dragonflies did their very best to treat others as they wished to be treated.

Only bats, birds, frogs and spiders posed any genuine threat. The spiders were sparse in numbers and therefore not a great worry. On the rare occasions when one was discovered, it would be destroyed quickly. The bats, like the birds, were avoided altogether, even the largest most fierce of dragonfly-kind wouldn't be a match for the smallest of either. As for frogs, all one need do was keep out of reach, problem solved.

***

131

"Ummm, hi!" Tuss said, as Auran finally approached. He still felt timid around his huge friend though Auran was always affable. The differences in age, size and experience left Tuss feeling awkward and nervous.

"Hello, Tussilago. It's been far too long since we've spoken, don't you think?"

"Yeah, it sure has. I'm sorry about that, I..." he began.

"Don't apologize. Life has its ups and downs and unusual courses to fly. I'm sure you're finding out for yourself. Today, our courses have crossed and for that I'm happy." Auran's rumbling voice always had a calming effect on Tuss.

Tuss' mind began to drift. He was trying to remember exactly when he'd last come to chat.

Auran cleared his throat, "Ehm, lost in your thoughts again?"

"Oops! Sorry. I haven't found a solution for that problem yet," Tuss answered sheepishly, "I'm working on it. I've tried Cas' patience on more than one occasion. That's not good, she can be tough!"

Deep laughter rumbled in reply. "Never stifle your imagination, not unless it gets you into trouble. And speaking of trouble, I've heard rumors about an impudent upstart of a young male dragonfly. One that's leading a rebellion against dragonfly-kind and all it holds dear and sacred."

Tuss was stunned. "Well, I..." he tried for a reasonable reply, but could only sputter out incoherencies.

Auran ignored his struggle and went on, "Would you happen to know who that might be?"

"No! I was...well, yes actually." Tuss wondered if his colors were showing his distress. He was completely off balance. Auran's rebuke was unexpected.

Laughter again. Auran was shaking all over. "Easy, lad. I shouldn't tease, but I couldn't resist the temptation. Please, forgive an old fliers' indiscretion."

"You were joking?" Tuss sighed with relief and laughed a little himself. "You had me worried "

"It seems as if you and Cas have taken my not so subtle hints seriously?"

"We sure have, Auran. But we never imagined things would turn out like this." He looked across the Fen to the east. "We were trying our best to keep the loneliness at bay, the games started by accident. Then it just grew and there are hundreds of dragonflies involved now. It's unbelievable! We had no idea!"

"That's one way to put it," Auran said. "You and your League have posed quite a problem for the more stodgy folk of dragonfly-kind. The Elders in particular have had quite a time of it. They've spent days pondering the changes, how they're to address it all. What you're doing is unprecedented. Not only do you ignore the old, ordered practices of Tradition; but you choose to do so in such a grand and open fashion, even risking dangerous exposure to our long-hated, winged nemesis."

"Yeah the birds, they're more aggravating than anything else. We set out watches, only a few of the foolish have fallen prey to them. We try and warn them and we never meant harm and I never intended to break the..."

"Tussilago, there's no need to be defensive around me. Don't take what I'm saying the wrong way. I think that what you and your cohorts have chosen to do is perfectly fine. You've not broken faith with the precepts that we hold dear. You've simply re-interpreted the way it happens to look on the outside." He paused long enough for his words to sink in, "and if you're willing to risk being eaten by birds in the process, well, that's certainly within your rights."

"I'm glad to hear you say that! We only wanted to stay together like before. If we did things how we were supposed to, I'd be half insane with boredom by now."

"I know Tuss, you've done no harm. In fact, I've heard about how your quiet friend Coria put the whole matter in proper perspective for the Elders." Auran laughed as he recalled the story, "I wish that I was there. They say it was a sight to behold and that even Salix was smiling by the time she was finished."

"You should've seen it! I stayed back, my presence might have caused more trouble than good, and they held their own anyway."

"They?" asked Auran.

"Yeah! Briza was in the middle of it, too. But it was Coria that won the day. She knows her Tradition, that's for sure."

"She sounds like the smart one."

"No doubt. She's a tough one too, a lot like Cas."

"Well then, I don't want to be the next to offend her. If half of what I heard about her is true."

"No worries. She's not that easy to offend. She puts up with an awful lot from, uh, from someone else." Tuss couldn't help but laugh. He could picture Coria giving Auran the business as she does with Briza.

The big dragonfly said, "Well, her speech had quite an impact on the Elders. I keep hearing dragonflies, young and old, talking about what she said. I've witnessed changes in even the most stubborn old timers and that's quite a feat for one so young to accomplish."

"Changes. What changes?" Tuss asked. "Besides the games?"

Auran chuckled. "Yes, the games and many more. I've renewed some old acquaintances; it's been too many years, long overdue. Do I need to emphasize how extraordinary a change that is?"

"No," said Tuss. "I know it's a big deal."

"Everyone seems eager, for lack of a better term, to be more social. There's a sense of community growing among the old-guard." He paused for a moment and watched as a mixed group of dragonflies flew through his area. They acknowledged Auran and Tuss with a friendly tip of their wings.

"My point exactly. What exquisite timing!" The two friends hovered in place and watched the high-spirited group go noisily on their way.

"Just a month or so ago, that little interaction would've devolved into a traditional confrontation. No one would get hurt of course, but times have changed and the folk of DragonTree have changed with them. I heartily approve, though something about it bothers me," His voice trailed off.

"Bothers you, Auran?"

"Don't be alarmed my dear Tussilago. It's probably nothing. Call it an old flier's concerns. I keep asking myself, why now? And what does it all mean?" Auran's usual, easy going demeanor had turned serious. "When the long held habits and traditions of a community change in one generation, there must be a reason. And if that's happening now, how will it affect us? Our history is replete with similar occurrences, all of them concerning major upheaval. We dragonflies seldom change our ways and most definitely, not very easily," He looked at Tuss, "So, I have to ask myself, what's the purpose of it all?"

Tuss gasped. Auran had just posed the same questions that he was grappling with. He fought to get his mental equilibrium back.

Auran noticed his extreme reaction. "Tuss, you don't look so well. Are you okay?"

"Yeah, I'm okay, but..."

It was Auran's turn to look troubled, "I meant no harm, Tuss. I was only speculating."

"I'm fine Auran. In fact, I'm better than fine. You surprised me is all, kind of caught me off balance. You've just asked the very questions that have bothered me for weeks. Maybe even since I emerged. It's at the heart of why I'm here right now."

"I see. Please explain."

"I'll try, but where to start."

"Take your time."

Time, yeah that's a good place. "Time's part of it Auran. So much has passed since we emerged. Do you really think after all this time, that there's a purpose?" Tuss didn't wait for an answer. He wanted to get it all out before he forgot anything. "See, we know we're very different, or strange, or something. Because we weren't like any of the hatches before us. We didn't set out to do things the way we have." A heavy burden lifted from him as he shared his thoughts and feelings. "Honestly, I've felt all along that I've had little choice in what's been happening. When I doubted what we should do next, I just followed my heart."

"Relax, Tussilago, I understand."

"Good! Because trying to put what I'm feeling into words, well," Tuss took a deep breath and continued, "Cas said there has to be a reason. Briza called it a purpose, too. Now you've said it and I wonder who else thinks it?"

"There are others. You young Tussilago, like it or not, were blessed to get there first, that's why it's been so onerous on you."

Tuss muttered, "I'm not so sure I want that kind of blessing, Auran."

"I don't blame you," Auran replied, "but in this, you're the one bearing the heaviest burden." He paused, "I've spoken with the Elders, so I know they've spent many days pondering the issue and discussing the likely ramifications. All we can conclude is that if change is coming, and you and your companions are at the center of it, we must wait for more revelation. And when or if it ever comes, we'll respond to it as best we can."

"That's exactly what Briza said. No one could argue the point with

Tussilago & Aurantium

him because it made sense. I'll tell him that he thinks like an Elder. He's going to love that."

The tension broken, they had a good laugh.

***

The day was bright and sunny, the two friends hovered companionably together, one brightly colored, thus far unblemished by time, one gray with age, his tattered wings a testament to the long life he'd lived. They shared a moment that both wished would last forever. The troubling concerns for the future were temporarily forgotten. The beauty of their home waters captivated them.

Auran finally spoke, "Enough of the serious talk, my young friend. I'm tired of speculation and what-ifs. The future will care for itself. We'll go crazy if we talk of nothing else. Let's proceed to something more pleasant, something easier on the mind and lighter on the heart. Why else, pray tell, are you here?"

Tuss had to consider. "Oh, yeah! I guess we stumbled into why. It's sort of the same subject. We've decided that our what-ifs as you put it, or maybe our purpose, is to explore the world outside the Fen. Do you see any problems with that?"

There was a long pause. Auran's eyes were inscrutable.

"I wish I could answer that for you, Tussilago. I don't want to disappoint you."

Tuss felt his excitement deflate. Had he come here only to get a non-answer?

"I've been a lonely dragonfly and have regretted that my generation has lived in solitude, but I never once felt compelled to change things as you have."

Is that supposed to be an answer? We went over that. Tuss wondered and then mumbled, "We didn't intend to change anything it just, sort of happened."

"But you and your friends did change everything, and as I said before, it's been for the good. I think though, that what you're wondering about now, is what's next."

"That makes sense, it fits with what we're feeling."

"It's as if you and your friends were born to search for what comes next. Your heart has propelled you forward and the results thus far, they've been wonderful. I only wish that I were younger, then maybe I could go myself," he sighed deeply. "Tussilago, here you are, asking me if it's okay to explore the greater world and what you fear most is the asking. Don't the unknowns that you might face out there bother you more?"

"No! My friends will be with me, what's out there for us to fear?"

"That's it exactly, my brave Tussilago," Auran said gently. "You have faith in your friends and that's a rare thing. Rarer still, your friends are worthy of that faith. I'm glad to be alive in the here and now, if only to have the pleasure of knowing you and one day soon, all of these great companions you've talked so much about."

"Thanks. I'll bring them here to meet you. It'll be noisy, but interesting too. Just not tomorrow. I want to go north and see the great swamp and beyond. What do you think of that?" Tuss asked.

"Are you asking for my opinion or for my permission? *Or* are you just telling me what your plans are?"

Tuss laughed, "I guess it's all three."

"Good then, I thought that was the case. Therefore, yes and no."

"Huh?" Tuss' laughter faded.

"Exactly!" replied Auran.

"What?" Tuss asked.

"Correct!" Auran said emphatically.

"I don't know what you mean, Auran. You're saying yes and no, but for which questions? Or whose questions, yours or mine? I'm confused."

"Exactly, Tussilago. I choose to be ambivalent with my answers. Don't think so hard about everything. Go, talk it over with your friends. Sleep on it, and then follow your heart. I think that Briza was correct; you'll know what to do when you're supposed to, circumstances will dictate, and choices will have to be made, some will be right, others wrong. Welcome to life!"

"Okay! I can accept that. It doesn't clear much up, but I think I understand your point. This is going to be just like before, when Cas and I decided to gather our friends and discuss our future. Except now, it won't be about whether or not we can still be friends. We'll be talking about what comes next, which is yet to be seen. Right?"

"Exactly! You knew the answers all along. It's good that you've told someone where you're going, though. I'll await your return and anticipate the stories you have to tell."

"Before I leave, I have one last thing I'd like to ask."

"You've my undivided attention. Ask away my young friend."

"When I was flying here, I was thinking about how big this part of the world is, how much there is to explore and that I've been ignoring it for too long. There are so many places I've never been. That's silly, isn't it?"

"That's not silly, that's something called youth, Tussilago. Life is complex. It's easy to be distracted. You've had your friends to focus on. Don't think yourself silly. Just enjoy the new revelations as they come. Pay attention to every detail and take joy in everything you can. When you go on your adventure, always think about what's happening around you and what it all means. Fly with eyes wide open and a heart that's willing to expand and grow. Live for every moment, Tussilago!"

"Thanks! I'll do my best, but..."

"You're welcome. But what?"

"You touched on it a while ago, Auran. Why me? Why am I the one who's always the first to become discontent?"

"You're a dragonfly of the DragonTree Fen, Tussilago. Daily you find yourself struggling against your very nature. The Fen's our home and we're tied body and mind to it. Our connections run deep, deeper than its darkest depths. This place is our life. We're born here. We live out our lives here. It's been so for generations, with Tradition acting as our constant guide, spanning all of the way back to Platanus and the great journey west."

Tuss had heard it all before, he waited patiently for his answer.

"You, unlike any other I've known, are not content with boundaries, you have eyes that stray beyond the familiar. When you look beyond the Fen and see the greater world, you realize that it has width and breadth undreamed of. For whatever reason, you feel drawn to seek what's beyond the borders of our beloved home. Therein dwells your conflict."

"But why me?" Tuss asked, "You said I'm brave and that you admire me for it, but I don't feel brave. I feel confused, lost and alone."

"But it's not just you, Tuss. You told me about Cas and Briza and I must assume the rest are feeling the same things. I surmise that they'll be bound up in whatever purpose you find."

"Oh! Oh, yeah. How could I forget? But still, when you said I *'get there first'*. Why? Why me?"

"Because you're a leader Tussilago. You'll come to that understanding one day. You've no choice in the matter; it's who and what you are. You were born with qualities that others admire and follow. You make choices when others waver, you move forward where others hesitate. You may have doubts but you do persevere and progress. "

"I'm not so sure that I like that role, Auran."

"I don't blame you, but if you have doubts about your leadership, just remember the changes you've wrought. This community has been blessed because you are who you are. That's all the proof you need, find confidence in that and be at peace. You've asked me if it's okay to go exploring. I was ambivalent with the answers but I can at least give you some direction."

"Anything would help," Tuss said, desperate for something to clasp on to.

"Wait until you hear what I have to say," he paused to consider, "Pay close attention to this for I fear what might happen to us if you don't follow your heart, Tussilago."

"What if my heart is wrong?"

"That's one possibility and yet to be discovered. After all, each of us is capable of making both good and bad choices. For now though Tussilago, trust a weary old dragonflies' intuition."

"Okay, I'll try. But, you're not that old Auran."

"You may be right, I've been spending time with old acquaintances from my pre-emergent life. We've been busy with our own distractions. We're tired and grumpy these days, sore and slow but even that's changing. That wouldn't have been possible before you. None of us would go back to how it was before."

"I saw you patrolling when I arrived. It seemed like a strange time for it. I wonder, does it have something to do with your new, how did you put it, distractions?"

Auran laughed, "I'll confess to nothing, you pert fellow. Now, off with you! I'm sure that you've enough to consider without worrying about my strange new habits and plenty to discuss with your friends as well," he paused and looked very stern. "Tussilago."

"Yes?" Tuss asked.

"Be safe! Would you? For me?"

"We will be, Auran."

"Oh, and before you go adventuring, please let me know exactly where you're going. You mentioned the north and the swamps, but I'd like to know for sure."

"Will do. Bye, Auran."

"Farewell my friend. Come back soon."

"I will."

Tuss flew away wondering if his friends would be angry with him. He'd promised to inform Auran of their future activities without asking them first. Briza might fuss, but that was to be expected. The others wouldn't have an issue.

And it's too late either way, I'm going to keep my word!

All that was left for Tuss to settle was; who would go and which direction, when they decided upon it.

Chapter Eleven

Somewhere Not Here

Tuss was worn out from the effort it took to explain everything to his friends. He spent the second half of the day telling them everything that he and Auran had discussed. It wasn't easy keeping things on track with Briza's constant interruptions. It could wear down even the most patient of dragonflies and Tuss was not the most patient. The *contributions* from the others didn't help either. They asked so many questions, Tuss couldn't be sure that he'd even told them everything. Auran was correct with his guess, all nine were going off to explore together. They were happy and excited about the possibilities. Cas was happiest of all, knowing that at least Auran would be aware of what they were up to.

Tuss had weighed the advantages and disadvantages of including Thymus and a couple other new members of the League, but in the end, decided against it. He knew that if this exploring-adventure thing was going to work, they'd need to keep the numbers of participants manageable. Others might create complications. The nine were close-knit, so the potential for unexpected troubles arising were minimal.

Tuss couldn't wait to get started, his friends would be by his side, and everything would be how it should be.

"So, where're we going?" Briza asked. "The northern swamp? You mentioned that before."

"Somewhere not here is good enough for me," Leon answered.

"That's an odd way to put it, but I like it," Coria laughed. "Anywhere not here works for me too."

"North then, into the swamp," Tuss agreed, "That's where Cas and I talked about going. We want to see what it's like up there, and find where it ends."

"That was easy enough. What time?" asked Gal.

"The first thing in the morning, first light. We can do our hawking on the way," Tuss answered decisively.

"What about our patrols," worried Mira, "And Auran knows that we're going?"

"I almost forgot. He did ask me about that and I said that we would let him know. You can stop looking at me like that, Briza, we're telling him. I gave my word. As for our patrols, we're going to be flying north from our areas anyway, so that'll more or less happen by default, right?"

"Oh, right. That's good thinking. But," Mira sounded worried, when everyone looked at her, she added, "never mind, I'm sure that everything will be fine."

"Good enough, then," said Aneth. "See you early. First it's Auran, and then it's into the unknown." He flew off without another word.

His departure sealed the plans.

"See you tomorrow," Briza said as he flew off, giving an enthusiastic shout to the evening sky.

"He's really looking forward to tomorrow," Gal said, laughing, "Good night."

Tuss and Cas said farewell to the rest as they flew off. They looked at each other and smiled with their eyes; nothing needed to be said. The next phase of their ever changing lives would begin tomorrow.

"Oh! I almost forgot to ask."

"What's that Tuss?"

"Who won the match?"

Cas answered him with a satisfied look and asked, "You realize that he avoided the whole subject while we were talking about heading north?"

"Yeah, I guess he hopes everyone forgets then? Congratulations are in order for you, Ace, Coria and Mira, eh?"

"Thanks! I'll fill you in on the details when I'm not so tired."

"I can wait."

They quietly hawked together, enjoying the peace of the evening. Once sated and perched Tuss asked, "About tomorrow, are we making a mistake?"

"If so, we'll be doing it together," Cas replied, "And that's good enough for me."

Chapter Twelve

Into The Swamp

Tuss was frustrated. He'd been through this very thing last evening. Their plans to start early were in jeopardy. It seemed like every dragonfly that'd ever flown in the games needed to be told why they should go about their daily routines and that he, Cas and the others would be back with them tomorrow. He wondered how they even knew that something was going on.

It was Thymus' well-timed arrival and input that sorted things out. He was very popular amongst the players and perfectly willing to use his strong personality to convince the few stubborn holdouts to leave Tuss and his group alone.

Thymus wasn't big or intimidating, but he had charisma, strength and was a natural leader. Tuss thanked him in private just before he left, taking the last of the more reluctant players with him.

Tuss had even asked if Thymus was interested in going; his answer was a very firm, "No thanks. Capture is adventure enough for me. I do appreciate being asked, though."

After watching the last of them vanish in the early morning mist, Tuss turned and found Cas and the others a short distance away. And that was when the next round of frustration began.

"But we'll only be a half days flight away," Briza protested.

"I know, but Tuss promised Auran," Cas shot back, "He won't rush to tell anyone else, and it's the smart thing to do."

"But," Briza started.

"And why complain now? You were told about this last night," Coria said, cutting off his next attempt to argue.

"I won't go anywhere unless someone back here knows about it," Gal said, clearly out of patience. "Cas and Tuss said that Auran is our friend and that's enough for me."

There was a short pause. Tuss was about to intervene. He was angry, not in the mood for another long and pointless debate.

Before he could speak, Briza relented. "You're right. I'm just anxious to get going."

"Good! I was afraid that we were gonna hover here all morning and argue. We won't go far if we do that, right?"

"Right Tuss, enough bickering. It's worn me out and I just woke up," Aneth sounded grouchy, which was usual. The effect was chilling. Anethum was Aneth's full name, and it meant strength; he was strong willed, honorable and huge. He wasn't quite as large as Auran yet, but he was close. When he spoke, dragonflies listened.

Tuss began to relax.

"That's settled then. Stay here, I'll be right back." Cas turned and sped towards the DragonTree.

"But..." Briza started to say.

"Too late Briza," Coria laughed. "She's already gone. She'll be right back and we can go."

"It's not funny. I just wanted to meet Auran is all."

"You'll get your chance soon enough," Tuss assured him. "Everyone will meet him when we get back. He'll want to know about everything."

"You said he didn't know what's beyond the Fen, didn't you Tuss?"

"Yeah, Gal. I think he knows more than he's told me, but maybe that's just me. He's intimidating, I mean, think of what he's seen in his life compared to our what, three moon phases?"

"Three and a half," Mira said, "Can you believe that?"

"Wow! No. How'd it take us this long to get so bored? We've spent our entire lives in this one small area." Briza was looking across the length of the Fen. The southern shore was lost in the thick, early morning mist rolling across the water. The sun would eventually burn it away, but for now everything was obscured. The usually spectacular panorama was cloaked in gray.

Tuss wondered just how misty the swamp would be. He didn't have the slightest idea. He'd never traveled beyond the first wide patch of reeds just north of where they were hovering. Until this moment, he'd hardly taken notice of how vast the reed field must be. He marveled at how he'd been able to ignore what was all around him for so long.

"The waiting's over. Here comes Cas," Ace said. She was excited, her voice was higher than usual and she was speaking quickly.

"Oh my! I guess it is," Mira didn't sound excited or happy, she sounded worried.

"This should be great fun," Coria said, her obvious enthusiasm was catchy.

"Done!" Cas shouted as she approached, "Auran's happy. We can leave without feeling any guilt."

"Hey! What do you think would happen if we just disappeared?" Briza asked.

"Briza!" Aneth said.

"You mean, for a day or so?" Mira's bright colors paled.

"Briza!" Aneth repeated before he could answer.

Briza heard the warning, "Never mind, Mira. Forget I asked. I was just trying to be funny, making another joke."

"A joke? That's an interesting way to put it," said Cas. "I'd say that you were being dimwitted and mean spirited."

"Well Cas, if you're going to act that way about it, I don't have to go."

"Don't, then!" she said. "You won't be missed, neither will your -foolishness."

"If that's how you feel."

"Briza!" Aneth repeated much louder this time. He was really angry. "Not another word. We all know you aren't going anywhere. And, what's the point joking right now?" He was in control of his temper, but just barely. "Don't answer that! Just let it go!"

"Yeah Briza, please let it go," Ace agreed. "Can't we just get started and try and have fun?"

Tuss felt his excitement fading. *Did it always have to be like this? Why can't his friends just enjoy each other's company without bickering? And why can't Briza try and not be Briza once in a while?*

"You're at an important juncture right now Briza, it's decision time," Cas said.

He looked at her, unable to decide exactly how to react to the uncomfortable situation he'd created. After a short pause, he relaxed and said, "Alright! You wanna have fun Ace? Here's how we'll do it, we'll forget what I just said and get going."

"I can't forget that easily. What'd you mean about us disappearing?" Mira persisted.

"Ummm..."

"Mira, does it really matter?" Tuss asked. "So what if we lose ourselves for a time? Sure, if we don't go, we won't be taking any risks. But then we're right where we were just a day ago, bored silly and wishing for change. How lost can we get? All of us know where home is, we feel it."

"You're right. I always know where home is, even at night or when the mist is so thick I can't see my wingtips," Mira mused.

"Are you having second thoughts, Mira?" Cas asked her.

"I was, but not anymore, thanks to Tuss," Mira answered. "It'd be easier to relax if Briza kept his more interesting thoughts to himself, though."

Everyone but Briza agreed with her.

"What about the rest of you? Coria? Leon?" Cas asked.

"I'm just wondering if we're ever going to get started," Leon answered.

"I'm ready," Coria said happily.

Tuss looked towards Cas, they locked eyes. She was ready to go, all arguments and conversations aside, the time had to come. He liked how easy it was for the two of them to talk without words.

Aneth must have been watching them and understood. He turned about and headed north. They flew out over the first long stretch of reeds and into the mist shrouded swamp.

Their first adventure together was getting underway.

Briza, seeing them leave, said, "I guess it's decided then."

Everyone else hurried to catch up. They hadn't gone far when the first of the large, cloudy pools of the lower swamp appeared below. The green thicket of the reeds ended, the morning mist roiled. A strange unexplored world opened before them.

A soft golden glow shone through the upper layers of mist as they left their well known, comfortable Fen behind. The very air they traveled through seemed to come alive and shimmer with radiance. This strange mixture of light, mist and new places created an atmosphere unlike anything they'd experienced before.

"Amazing!" Tuss said in a whisper, "And it's just the beginning, the promise of change and excitement, the end of days that run together. This will be anything but boring!"

"Yeah," Cas whispered back, filled with the same awe.

The bickering and unanswerable questions were left behind them.

They were together and beginning something new. No one would forget this moment. It was filled with excitement, wonder and enough fear to sharpen the senses.

Tuss was thrilled, he felt so alive. He knew that they were doing the right thing, his heart told him so, the reactions of his friends told him so. They were flying headlong towards the unfamiliar, towards change, ready to face life's next challenge, and doing so together.

Tuss shouted, "Finally! We get to see some of the rest of the world."

"Yeah, into the unknown," Cas agreed, her voice whimsical.

Briza shouted back excitedly. "Hey yeah! We're not in the Fen any more Tussilago!"

***

They didn't see the shapes following at a distance nor did they feel the eyes watching them.

Third needed to inform the Queen. She reached across the distance, touched the group-mind and heard; *nothing.* The Queen's commanding presence was still absent. Third's latest report would have to wait. She focused back on the prey.

Gone! Lost in the mist...

***

Several butterflies had been flitting about the fields that bordered the swamp. It was much quieter in the north, far from the noisy disruption caused by the silly dragonflies. Their usual browsing grounds had become the center of the obnoxious creatures raucous activities, chasing them to more out-of-the-way locales. Keeping distance from others, remaining detached and seeking peace was their way. The Butterfly Creed stated: *"Separate ourselves from others, avoid unnecessary interactions, if something does not affect us directly, dismiss it. We do not interfere."* They observed, remembered, lived and let live. Actual contact with other creatures was to be avoided.

For one of them, however, the strictest adherence to those aspects of the Creed was decreasing with each passing day. She was troubled by the repeated appearance of the strange invaders. Watching them spy upon the creatures of the Fen and the dragonflies in particular, worried her.

Speyeria-Idalia had listened as the nine had their meeting under the large tree on the west side of the Fen. She saw the bees that day too when she wandered north to the swamp's edge, seeking peace and quiet.

Another strange coincidence this has been, I have to say! The thought troubled her. The bees were intruders, very unusual ones, with an air of mortal danger about them. The dragonflies could be much the same, fierce and deadly, though for generations, they'd chosen to live peacefully, until recently.

Odd behavior on the bee's part and odd behavior by the dragonflies of late, hmmm, yes! Idalia thought. *This is very strange indeed. I must consider the possible implications. I must continue to observe and remember.*

What is that? Speyeria-Nokomis asked, as he flew over and joined her on the cluster of brilliant purple, star shaped flowers. He'd heard her thoughts. His arrival surprised her; she'd wandered far from him, he must have followed.

"Oh, nothing. Nothing at all," she said. She liked to practice her speech when she could. Nokomis was the only butterfly that would actually talk with her. "I was just observing the behavior of strange creatures, so to say. They arouse my curiosity, for they watch in secret."

"Your curiosity, Idalia? The heart of your troubles. What is interesting about obnoxious dragonflies? Silly through and through, interesting only as they behave differently. Groups of them, acting foolish."

"Not them, Nokomis. Others have come at various times and they trouble me deeply. They lurk in the shadows."

"Listen as I say our Creed, Idalia. Observation is enough for observation's sake, it's what we do and all that we do," Nokomis sounded impatient. "It's not our place to interfere, change happens, we're to watch and remember, and only that."

"I know our beliefs. We sleep, eat and breathe the Creed. We never interfere, and we do not interact. We go about our business and observe, so to say."

"Correct, we should focus on that alone, Idalia. How far north you have come and only to trouble yourself over such a silly matter."

"It's not silly! I shall though, refocus for now, as you say. But I will keep my doubts," she answered, "And Nokomis, I came north seeking quiet, the trouble was here before me."

"I'm corrected! My apologies Idalia. Peaceful, yes, it's peaceful here, let's remain for a time."

They browsed the flowers that flourished abundantly all through the rolling fields bordering the swamp. A fast running stream meandered its way through the area. Together they alighted on the shore and puddled with a flurry of white and black Zebra Swallowtails. Other than pleasantries, no information was exchanged; but each species closely observed the other.

Idalia's concerns wouldn't allow her anxious mind to rest. She tried her best to enjoy the day, but her thoughts clashed together. *If circumstances were normal, I could be at peace. But they are not and*

Nokomis & Idalia

therefore I'm uneasy. Try as she might she couldn't do as Nokomis suggested and focus on the peaceful aspects of their beliefs. *The Creed is correct I know, but what if blindly, unquestioningly following how others have defined it, hurts us? And what if that hurts others?*

She looked about, Nokomis was a distance from her, the worry welled up and she spoke aloud, letting her voice vent what concerned her most of all. "When and how did our rules begin to take precedence over the welfare of others?"

These were questions that Idalia had no answers for. She wasn't sure she wanted answers. They could be dangerous things. The life she'd lived had always been a happy one, if not mundane. The world's natural machinations worked in favor for her kind. Therefore, how could she not be happy? She knew that she should be. But there was one nagging thought, no matter how hard she tried to ignore it, that wouldn't allow her troubled mind to rest. *If we see something wrong and do nothing about it, nothing to stop it, what does that say about us?*

Chapter Thirteen

Through The Mist

Tuss was having the time of his young life. He could barely make out the shapes of his friends spread all around him. They were flying through the golden mist over the strange, ever-changing landscape. They'd just passed over what he guessed was the last of the open channels of reed lined waterways. He was seeing solid ground that sprouted very dense growths of various, unusual plants.

Tuss figured that they were flying due north, the lack of clear skies hadn't affected his sense of direction. He could feel where north was. It wouldn't hurt to have a look at the sun though. Once that happened there'd be no doubt about their exact heading.

He was deep in thought, wondering about how big the world might actually be. Home was far-far away and here he was, surrounded by strange shapes, sights and sounds..

Cas' voice startled him. "It'd be easy to get lost up here." She'd flown up right alongside him without his noticing. "Mira's fears could be realized, if we're not careful."

"You keep doing that!" he said.

Cas laughed, "and you keep letting me! I like making you start."

"I need to pay more attention to what you're doing and deprive you of the pleasure."

"You should certainly try, Tuss. Otherwise, you're going to fly straight into a tree or something worse without realizing it."

"You'd like to see that, wouldn't you?"

"Nah, I like the way you look, a tree would alter that too much. So, what do you think, Tuss?"

"Think about what? My good looks or what else?"

"No! Don't make me regret the compliment. What I was asking is; wouldn't it be easy to get lost up here?"

"Oh, yeah! No doubt, except," He paused.

"Except what?"

"Except, like I said before. I can feel where we're going and I can feel where home is and where the DragonTree is, even from all the way up here. How odd is that?"

"Not odd at all, Tuss, I think I know what you…"

"GOTCHA!" Briza shouted, surprising them. He'd tagged Cas and flown off quickly, zigging and zagging his way through the tangles of plants, laughing the entire time.

"Looks like you're it!" Tuss shouted, even as he veered away from her.

Cas was up for the game, too. "I'm coming for you, Briza and I'll get you! You can't fly fast enough or far enough, so laugh while you can."

"Oh yeah!" Briza shouted back to her, "we'll see about that."

Surprise me once, okay, but let's just see how long it lasts, she thought to herself as she poured on speed, rapidly catching up with the two laughing fools. Flying like this through the strange landscape made it impossible for Cas to contain her own excitement, she let go of any doubts and her own laughter rang out. She was happy. They were all together, flying into the unknown, embarked upon a grand adventure.

***

It wasn't long before all nine of them were swooping in a whirl of blazing colors, streaking through the golden air cutting intricate patterns into the mist. As they chased each other through the dense growth of reeds and strange stands of water plants, they lost all track of time and direction.

Tuss was happy to be young and part of this adventure. He watched as his friends adapted quickly to the new environment. The saturated landscape was nothing like the eastern meadows. The impromptu game of Tag had begun cautiously. The first few moments of the chase had been met with some hesitance. Soon enough however, once they had a feel for the unfamiliar environment, all caution was thrown to the wind. The simple game had evolved into a wild and merry chase.

Time and distance went unnoticed as they played their way through the stunted trees and brushy thickets. They instinctively headed north, the air growing cooler as they progressed. The excitement of playing one of their favorite games in an unusual place was too much fun to bother with concerns like weather conditions and temperatures.

As the wild activity went on and on, Tuss began to realize that they weren't really exploring any more. The thought didn't bother him as much as he would have suspected and either way, they were having fun. That counted for something. He rationalized that they could explore and play at the same time. And as soon as that thought occurred to him he found his mind changing. He began to slow down.

Cas flew up beside and said, "There really isn't that much to see up here, is there? Everything looks the same to me. It's a thick, foggy, green, brown and wet world. I can hardly tell one spot from another."

"Yeah. And have you noticed that the mist is getting thicker? I can hardly see past a few wing beats. The glow of the sun is all but gone, too."

"Is that why you just slowed down?"

"Not just that, Cas. I was enjoying the game at first but it occurred to me that we've come all this way without paying attention to where we're going. That's okay, we can play and explore at the same time, but now I'm feeling strange, like there's something else. Something ahead maybe?"

"Me, too. I don't like the idea of flying straight into the trunk of one of these trees either," Cas answered.

Briza flew up behind the two at that moment and asked, "I take it that the game's ended?"

"I suppose so, Briza, sorry."

"S'okay, it was great while it lasted, and we can come back later."

"Whoa! Hold up! Come look at this. Wow! I can hardly believe what I'm seeing!" It was Leon, and he sure didn't sound like the Leon they knew. His voice was raised in alarm, almost panicked.

The game was over, the fun forgotten. They reacted just as they would in the eastern meadows to the cry of "Break, break!" Their senses were alert for danger.

He was hovering in place, facing south and waiting for them with bright eyes whirling. His colors were a burning contrast to the dim and gray world around him.

"I'm not imagining this, am I?"

A gentle breeze stirred the thick mist as he asked his question. It thinned and revealed an imposing wall of rock just behind him. It rose up out of sight. His tight posture as he hovered communicated that he was looking for both confirmation and comforting. As they drew nearer to him, he turned back to look at what they'd discovered.

After a long breathless pause, Briza finally answered, "No, you aren't imaging it Leon. We see it too!" He looked at the rest of the group to ask, "Right?"

"Wow, oh wow," Mira muttered, "That's something else!"

"That's the biggest thing I've ever seen," Tuss said. His words sounded strange even to himself. "It's just a bunch of rock after all, but the shear size and scope of it!"

"Hmmm!" muttered Gal.

The nine friends hung there speechless.

Looking at the seemingly endless rampart of solid rock made Tuss feel small. *The world is so big! And I'm just a simple dragonfly from a small place.* He strained his eyes, looking as far as he could see, both east and west. There was no end to the immensity. He looked up. What he could see in that direction was just as impressive and incomprehensible to him. The wall climbed jaggedly past the tallest treetops, disappearing into the mist.

"Well, there's no denying it. This is the sort of thing that we set off to discover," Briza said, breaking the silence. They were in awe.

"Wow! Just wow!" Ace said, echoing Mira's initial reaction. She wasn't alone. Now that Briza had spoken, everyone except Tuss had plenty of comments and they all began to talk at once.

Cas shushed them. Once quieted she asked, "What do you think, Tuss?"

"It's big," he said.

"Now if that isn't the understatement of our lives, I don't know what is," laughed Briza.

"He's right though," Coria said in Tuss' defense.

"Well, duh! But come on, Coria! This's more than just big, it's...it's amazing!" Briza retorted.

Coria harrumphed and flew away from everyone. She began to ascend the rock face. It didn't take long for her to rise up above the lower tree canopy.

Gal spoke up, "Hey, Coria!" His tone was sharp and commanding, causing her to stop and look back. "Come down, would you?" Concern increased in his voice with every word he spoke.

Dragonflies had limits, their flying abilities were great, but even the strongest flier had to be careful. They could only go so high. Coria was just about to fly past those limits and Gal's timely call had stopped her just short of certain danger. It was odd behavior for Coria. She was always so levelheaded. She glanced back up, glanced back at them and then took another longer look up. They could see that she was struggling to make a decision.

"Come on, Coria!" Mira and Ace said at exactly the same time. She heard them, but their pleas held little sway. She looked east and west, allowing her gaze to take in the cliff face as far as she could see. She acted like she was entranced.

She seemed to Tuss to be lost and confused. He'd seen enough. "Stay put, I'm going to get her back!" He flew up towards her as fast as he could. When he got close, he could hear her talking distractedly.

"This makes even the DragonTree seem small." She sounded distant and strange, "I wonder if it's possible to fly up over it?"

"NO!" Tuss shouted. He was very close. He looked down and felt a tremor of fear run through him. He'd never been so high before. Not even that first day when the bird nearly had him. When he saw her ascending once more, he again shouted "NO!"

Coria stopped and spun around to face him. She looked scared but there was something he'd never seen in her eyes before; there was hurt. Tuss had never raised his voice at her before. He felt bad about doing it just now, but he knew he'd feel worse if she flew any further and was dashed against the rocks by a strong gust of wind.

"Sorry to shout Coria, but I don't think this is a good idea. You aren't acting quite yourself at the moment. Look around you!" She did. "Now look down. We're pretty high don't you think? What else tends to fly this high?"

She shook herself; it was like watching her wake her up. "Birds and bats. Oh! Oh my! Tuss! What was I thinking?"

"Good, you're back. What you were thinking doesn't matter right now. Let's hurry up and get back down to the others. When we get there, we can talk it over, but not way up here."

She broke eye contact with him for just a moment and looked upwards. Her voice grew distant again, "It's okay Tuss, I just need to fly up the cliff and see what's beyond."

Tuss' dismay was growing with each passing moment. *This is a strange place, it's no wonder strange things are happening.* Everything felt wrong. Something was pulling him forward too. Whatever it was, up above and out of sight was extremely compelling. He knew what she was feeling now. He wanted to fly with Coria. Together, they could go and see what was up beyond the mist.

"Here now, I'll go with her." It was Briza and he sounded more excited than ever, "Just wait here, Tuss. We need to give it a good try now that we've flown all of this way. Just wait while the two of us..."

Tuss was frozen in place, confused, speechless. He was frightened and didn't know why, and not knowing frightened him even more. He wanted to go with them, but knew deep down inside that it would be a mistake. *This isn't what I was thinking about when I suggested we come here exploring.* Something had to be done, and quickly, or they'd fly off together into the dangerous unknown. How could he stop them when he wanted to go himself?

"What do you say Coria, we go together?"

"Yeah!"

"No," Tuss said again, unable to put any power or conviction into his voice. They stopped and looked at him. "Just wait, let me think, I need time to think!"

Young dragonflies of the Fen perished every year by foolishly taking and making dares, trying to fly the highest. Once grabbed by upper level winds it was all over. No matter how strong they were, the winds were stronger. They could be deadly and unforgiving. Even a modest upper-level gust could tear a dragonfly's wing apart. Tuss had actually seen it happen and all because of a ridiculous challenge. He never wanted to see anything like it again. He could picture it in his mind, Coria or Briza being blown into the rocks and broken, or losing their wings to the winds one at time, as they struggled against the inevitable. Those images broke his paralysis.

"Stop! Both of you please stop!" His voice sounded weak. He realized that fear for what might happen to his friends was robbing him of his strength. They would never listen.

"STOP NOW!" Aneth said, his voice rumbling up from far below, echoing all around, bouncing off the rock wall. "You've not thought this through. Come back immediately. STOP THIS FOOLISHNESS, NOW!"

Tuss was shocked back into his right mind by Aneth's anger. The others were yelling now, too. Tuss could hear genuine fear in every word.

Coria and Briza stopped and turned back, eyes clearing.

Aneth's voice had that kind of effect. When he spoke the way he just had, none could ignore it. Tuss watched over the two as they flew down to the worried group. He fell in behind, making sure there'd be no further changes of heart.

Aneth waited until they were close enough for him to speak without shouting, "What's wrong with you two? I can't see the top of those cliffs from here, and I'm sure it's getting darker, look at the sky. Didn't you notice?" He gave them time to look around and see the deeper shades of gray that darkened the mist. "And as strong as I am, I wouldn't have a chance of surviving up there...the winds, you know."

"Oh," Briza said, "I didn't consider that."

"Me, either," Coria's voice sounded normal. "I wasn't thinking clearly just now. It's like I was someone else, disconnected and watching. When I heard Tuss' voice it was like something from a dream, not really real. Easy to ignore."

"Me too, Coria. Something just got to me and it was very compelling."

"Can we talk about that later? Aneth's right, look how dark everything is." Mira's worry was contagious. "You could've been eaten by birds as high as you were but even they're smart enough to stay in cover when a storm's coming."

"Yeah," was all that Tuss could say. He wanted to thank Aneth for what he'd just done but he couldn't find the voice to do it. The image of losing his friends was still too fresh in his mind.

"There's no doubt about it," Gal said. "It looks like it's getting late right now, but we know better. Do any of you feel like I do, that it's far too dark, way too early?"

"I do Gal," Cas agreed. "It may be a bit after midday, but it shouldn't be this dark."

"We should head back." Mira sounded upset.

"Go back now?" Briza didn't sound happy. "Why? We just got here. We should explore as much as we can. It's not that late. We just left the Fen a little while ago, right?"

"No, we left the Fen half a day ago," Gal informed him. "We were so wrapped up in our playing that we completely lost track of time."

"We couldn't have lost track that much, could we?"

Cas began to laugh.

"What?" Briza asked.

"Oh, nothing really, it's just funny is all. Here we are in a strange place that none of us has ever been to. And yet, for some reason, all of us feel kind of the same way about it. Like there's something familiar about it, or maybe something we should be doing that we haven't quite figured out yet. That's why the two of you flew off so eagerly, ready to risk your lives for who knows what."

"But why's that funny, Cas?" Mira didn't see what Cas found so humorous in their present situation.

Cas continued, "It just is. For whatever reason, we wanted to abandon caution and fly away into the unknown, I know I did. We all did and still do. Am I right?"

Everyone but Mira agreed.

"Briza and Coria must feel whatever it is more strongly than the rest of us. But Gal's right. It's getting darker. Something is stealing the day's light from the sky. We played most of the morning away while we flew north. You know what it's like to get caught up in the fun of a game. All of us joined in and we just ignored the time."

"Hey now! You seemed willing enough to play along, all of you did," Briza sounded defensive. Tuss hoped an argument wouldn't break out.

Aneth must have noticed his petulance too. "No doubt about it, Briza. All of us got lost in the fun. You didn't force us to play, but we did, and lost track of time. Cas was simply pointing out why it's later then we realized. No one's casting blame on anyone."

Good, thought Tuss, *Aneth sure knows how to manage their sometimes-troublesome friend.*

"Aneth's right, Briza. And even if I did want to lay blame it would be on all of us. It doesn't matter though. We had a lot of fun. It made the journey interesting. If we didn't play our way up, it would've been a boring trip," Cas said.

Tuss was grateful for both Aneth's and Cas' intervention. He wondered if it might not be a bad idea to pull Briza aside from the others once they'd returned home and talk to him about the increasing frequency of his tirades.

"Okay, good enough then," Briza finally said, "I still don't see what you find so funny about all of this, Cas."

"It's not funny, as in *ha-ha* funny. It's *really strange* funny instead. I probably shouldn't laugh but I'd rather do that than panic." She let out a sigh, "but enough of that. We played around for how long? Most of the morning, right? So yeah, it can't be that late, just like you said."

"Right, half the morning, but no longer." Tuss' inner senses were telling him more than his outward senses. "I'm only just now starting to get hungry which means it's not long past mid-day. If it were evening, I'd be starved. What about the rest of you?"

They agreed.

"I wish that we could see the sun, just to be sure," Mira said, looking around at the dark, gloomy mist that masked even the lower branches of the trees. A sudden, bright flash electrified the world all around them. A loud booming clap of thunder followed almost immediately. It was so unlike the blazing lights they'd watched streaking across the night sky not so long ago and yet, somehow the same. Both phenomena came from high above, were grand, beautiful, fear inducing and filled them with wonderment.

Thunder boomed again, none saw the lightning that proceeded it, which was a very bad sign.

Everyone reacted.

"Uh oh!" said Gal. "That's not good."

The mist was stirred by a gust of wind. There was another flash of lightning, this one even brighter than the last. The thunder that followed was near deafening and then the vibrations rattled them as the sound bounced off the cliffs.

"That one was too close!" Ace said.

They were stunned.

"Oh great," Coria muttered, "we know what that means." She didn't sound worried, just annoyed.

Well, that's Coria, not afraid of anything, just practical and straight to the point. Tuss had to hide his laughter. The smallest of his friends was probably the bravest. Not even the confrontation with the Elders scared her. So why would any storm?

"We better find some shelter and fast," Aneth said as the first fat drops of rain started to fall around them, "this's going to be a bad one."

"How did we miss this one coming on?" Cas asked as they began to fly in search of a safe place to shelter. "The big ones like this always announce themselves ahead of time, with lots of wind, usually."

"The cliffs must be blocking the worst of it," Gal offered. "Being this close to them, there's no way we could know if it was coming down from the north. We're not as exposed here as we are at the Fen. This area isn't as flat and wide open."

Leave it to Gal to offer the logical answer. For whatever reason, he just knew things. Tuss couldn't help but envy his friend a little.

"I think we were a little distracted thanks to Coria and Briza."

"Forget that for now, would you Leon?" Tuss asked, hoping to avoid what could be another poorly timed argument. He looked at Briza, who was focusing all his attention upwards.

"I guess that this really means we won't be trying to find the clifftops just yet?" Briza actually sounded disappointed.

Tuss couldn't believe what he was hearing. "Briza, after all we were just talking about and you still need to ask that? With a bad storm coming?"

Cas cut Tuss off. She was furious now. "What! Are you joking? Come on Briza, get serious, if you want to explore right now, why not go and discover a nice and safe place that'll keep us out of the downpour that's coming."

"Okay! We'll go later, after the storm." He wasn't joking. He sounded half dazed again.

Tuss wanted to go and knock his friend out of the air and leave him out in the rain as a lesson. "Briza..." he began.

"Don't start on me, Tuss. I know I'm aggravating everyone right now, but there's a good reason to forgive me."

"Oh yeah?" Cas asked, even as she moved closer to him. Tuss started towards her. She might really have it out with him, right here and now.

"Yeah! I've already found a nice spot for us, at least I believe so." His voice was casual, not dazed any longer. "The rain must be thinning the mist. I couldn't see any details over there just a short bit ago, but now I'm pretty sure I'm seeing what looks to be a big opening in the rocks. What do you say?"

"Where?" Cas stopped to look. Tuss almost bumped into her.

"There, just to the left of that sharp outcropping, near the base of the cliffs. Follow me." Briza started to move to where he was indicating. The rain began to pound down even harder. Flying was difficult. Soon enough they would be knocked out of the air by the heavy torrents if they didn't get to safety.

"Oh no! Not a cave," Mira groaned.

"We don't have a choice, Mira. I can hardly stay in the air as it is," Ace said as she closely followed Briza.

"I don't see anything better, Mira, not if we want to get out of this storm any time soon." Tuss tried his best to keep his voice steady. He didn't like the look of the cave, either.

"I guess if there's no other choice."

They moved in a group, following Briza, towards the shadowy opening. When they got close Tuss could see it more clearly. It looked to him like a giant, gaping mouth. Much like those of the fish that inhabited the deeper waters of the Fen, always ready to make a meal out of any dragonfly foolish enough to get stuck on the surface. He shuddered with the thought. As a nymph, he'd narrowly escaped from one of those underwater monsters on more than one occasion. And since he'd emerged, he'd heard stories about those large fish pulling hapless creatures under. Chills ran through him. *Why,* he asked himself, *did I have to call to mind those kinds of memories at a time like this? I better not say what I'm thinking out loud. Briza would probably love it, Mira would be terrified and Gal might have some horrible details to add about how fish digested food.*

"Ick! I don't like this place at all," Mira said, even before she entered. "Let's find something better, okay?" She started to move away from the cave entrance, panicked.

"It's too late for that now," Aneth comforted. "Stay close Mira, we'll be fine."

It was too late. The sky opened and the pounding rain fell even harder. If they went out into the open they would be washed out of the air. If they were lucky and weren't swept into the swamp waters, they'd have to spend the storm however long it lasted without shelter. It was possible to survive on a log or a tree, maybe even on a rock if they could get to it, but they would be battered and pummeled mercilessly in the process. It would be terribly uncomfortable at best. None of them knew exactly what lived in the swamps, though frogs were a certainty, and none cared to find out whatever else dwelt there.

"Mira!" Tuss warned. She was moving towards the opening despite what Aneth had just said.

"I know. We have to stay here now. Don't worry Tuss, there's no way I'm going out there now, no matter how much I dislike this cave. But, I'm staying as far from the dark as I can safely get."

"Good enough, then."

The friends hovered in place, watching the rain pour down, the cold throat of the cave stretched behind them to who knows where.

"Just look at that. Have you ever seen it rain like that before?" Coria asked, moving even closer to the entrance. She landed on a jut of rock next to Mira, just far enough inside the overhanging roof so that the water didn't splash on her. She knew that keeping dry meant staying warm. They had to preserve their body heat if they wanted to fly later.

Cold was an ever present concern. If they chilled too much, they wouldn't be able to fly comfortably. If they got really cold, they wouldn't be able to fly at all.

Tuss had a troubling thought. He wondered if the great cliffs blocked the noonday sunlight and warmth. It was already after midday when they'd arrived here and the mist was still thick. Did it ever thin? Did the sun burn it off in this swampy region, ever?

Here they were though, in the north, far from home, stuck in a strange cave, waiting for a powerful storm to end.

Time passed slowly as the tempest raged on.

***

The rain beat down. Tuss looked outwards from the cave's mouth wishing it would end. He was perched with his friends which was good but there was that word again, *mouth*. *I better think of it as a cave opening from now on. Forget the whole idea of hungry mouths*. He was begging his mind and active imagination to give him peace, *just this once.*

Briza spoke excitedly, breaking the silence, "Are any of you thinking what I'm thinking?" His voice became fainter as he spoke.

Tuss turned to see why he sounded so odd. Briza had flown deep into the cave. His form was all but invisible in the low light.

"Hey! What're you doing?" Ace yelled into the cave, her voice cracked with fear.

171

Mira in the Cave

"Don't say it Briza, please!" Mira squeaked out.

"Briza, come on now! Why?" Cas asked unnecessarily. All of them knew what was on his mind. They knew that he was ready to fly off into the dark. And it was just like Briza to do it without giving safety any consideration. It was a repeat of what had happened outside.

"You're on your own this time!" Coria shouted to him. Even though she'd been ready to try and fly over the cliffs, she felt no desire to go into the dark cold depths of the earth.

"Please come back! You're just a shadow, I can barely see you," Ace pleaded.

"I'm okay, really!" Briza said, his voice growing even fainter as he flew further in.

"I'm not going in there, no way, no how and that's final!" Mira kept her voice under control, but just barely.

"No worries, Mira. None of us are flying any deeper into this cave!" Aneth's voice was comforting. "You're coming back right now, aren't you Briza?"

Everyone waited for his answer.

"Ummm. I, uhhh..."

"Briza!"

"Yeah right, okay Aneth," he finally answered to the relief of everyone. He didn't sound as disappointed as before, "it's too dark and too cold anyway. I wouldn't be able to fly for long, but there's just something about it." His voice grew louder and clearer as he came back.

"Now that's a good dragonfly!" Aneth said. "No sense in splitting up now, not this late in the day, isn't that right Briza?"

"No doubt!" Briza agreed absently. He was looking back into the cave; he didn't sound very happy or very confident.

Tuss wondered if he was afraid of something he had seen or felt.

Briza settled on the rock. He was struggling to keep his eyes and attention from straying back.

"So, it's decided then. We wait out the rain right here. It shouldn't be too long and we've Briza to entertain us since he hasn't lost himself in the dark," Gal joked. "What's next, Briza? Are you planning to take a trip to the stars tonight? Are you off to fly around the moon, just for the fun of it?"

Briza didn't have an answer; he kept staring into the depths and remained quiet for the time being.

More time passed and the storm raged on.

"There must be an opening somewhere else. I can feel a steady draft," Gal turned to them and said after a time. "I mean, if the air is moving towards us from under ground and passing out through the cave opening, it has to be replaced by air feeding in from someplace else."

"Is this the right subject to be discussing at the moment?" Tuss asked him.

"Why not, we're here, the cave is here and it'll pass the time. Okay, Tuss?"

"Yeah, but..." He looked at Briza.

"I'm interested in what he has to say, Tuss," Aneth said. "Briza, you stay put on your own, or I'll make you. Got it?"

"Yeah, whatever Aneth," he replied laughing, "go on Gal."

Everyone looked at Gal with interest.

"Now, I haven't been underground before, and I'm pretty sure that none of you have either, right?"

"Right," they answered.

"Okay. So we're only speculating here but I think it makes sense. Wouldn't it be something if we had enough light to go through from this end and find out where the other opening is? My guess is that this cave leads somewhere else, somewhere above ground. The moving air we're feeling has to be coming from someplace."

"Yeah it must be coming down from above, some place over the cliff top," Briza, his mind back from where it had wandered, said. "We've got to go see if Gal's right!"

"Oh not again! Give it a rest, would you, Briza?" Tuss spoke up angrily. He hated to speak to anyone in anger, and this was the second time this afternoon. It worked; Tuss had Briza's full attention. *Once again, I find myself shouting and angry. What an adventure this is turning out to be.*

"Alright, alright! I'll give it a rest. Calm down Tuss. I'm done with it," Briza said. He couldn't hide his disappointment. "I'm not going anywhere for now, but I don't know why you..."

"Think about it from our perspective Briza," Cas cut him off in a matter-of-fact voice, "We had to argue and plead with you just a little while ago. You were about to risk your life and go flying up and away to who knows where. Then we had to argue with you to get you out of the storm. Now you want to fly into the dark, hoping to arrive somewhere outside safe and sound. Look outside, see that rain? Imagine if we were high above the cliffs, out there in the wide open. Think about the gusting winds that usually spring up just before the rain begins to fall." She paused, hoping that what she was saying would sink into his stubborn mind. "None of us know anything about this cave. Gal has just pointed out that maybe, not for sure, but maybe there's another way in or out of here. That could mean anything, you know. Oh and one more thing you may not have considered. What might be living in there?"

"Oh my!" Mira said rising from her perch, ready to fly out into the storm.

"Don't say things like that!" Ace said. She looked as worried as Mira but remained perched close to Aneth.

Cas ignored them and continued, speaking directly to Briza, "Have

175

you even thought about that? Don't bats live in caves?" Everyone shuddered and looked for their nighttime nemeses. The very mention of them at a time like this was unthinkable. The bats of the Fen region would eat dragonflies if given the opportunity. If there were any here in the north, they wouldn't be any different.

"Alright, alright!" Briza said, chastened. "I'm not going anywhere, I promise."

Lightning flashed, the following thunderclap ended all conversation for a time.

They perched and waited, the air cooled further and more rain poured down.

"Cave, what is it about a cave," Gal muttered, breaking the long silence. "There's some mention about caves in one of the old stories."

"Oh! I remember something too, or I almost do."

"Me too, Cas," Aneth said, "It has something to do with travel."

"Gal, is it the one about Platanus?" Tuss asked. "If so, it's probably my all time favorite."

He nodded. "Yes, that's the one. It's about how our ancestors first found the Fen and the DragonTree, and how they fought to make it their home. I seem to recall the mention of a cave far to the north. Platanus had to go through it to find whatever it was that he and his folk needed."

"I remember that too, but how did they get through the cave in the story? I doubt we could go very far in this one. There isn't much light and even with the full sun shining there'd hardly be more. Far too many of the stories we were told are missing a lot of major details."

"That's the most I've heard you say at any given time, Leon."

"Knock it off, Briza, he's right!" Cas said.

"But it's true, Cas! He hardly ever strings more than a couple words together."

"Yeah Briza, you're right, I don't speak much. But conversely, you speak far too much and actually say so little of worth," Leon replied. Everyone but Briza laughed.

Instead of reacting to being bettered in the war of words, he chose to ignore the insult as if it never happened, "But, I wonder if that story has something to do with my inexplicable need to explore this cave? Do you think this could be the very same cave?" asked Briza.

"I've no idea. I'm glad you've finally given up trying to go through it though," Cas said. "I thought for a bit there that Aneth would have to physically stop you."

"Yeah Briza, really!" Coria added. "I was ready to ask Gal and Leon to help him pin back your wings."

"Hey!" Ace said, "I wouldn't mind getting back to what Gal was saying. It was something about the reasons for Platanus going in the first place. Do any of you know any more about why?"

"That's strange. It should've occurred to me to ask ages ago, when we were in class. I never did," Leon said, "and I loved the history stories, probably as much, if not more, than anyone."

"No doubt!" Tuss laughed. "We practically had to drag you away from classes back then. You drove the poor Teachers mad with all the questions you asked. Back then you spoke to them a lot more than you did to us. It's funny how none of us asked more about Platanus though, me especially since he's my favorite character from history."

"You know, I've no idea why I didn't, either," Gal added. "From what I remember, the story we did get wasn't very complete. That should've piqued my curiosity more."

"I asked once," Briza said, his voice sounding dreamy and distant.

"You? I'm surprised, Briza."

"Yeah me, Gal, and the only kind of answer I got was, '*It's none of your concern. We've told you what you need to know, so focus on something which actually matters...*' or, something to that effect. Can you believe it? I finally show an interest in something having to do with class and learning and they brush me off. I wish now that I'd kept asking until I had the answers. The curiosity is going to drive me crazy."

"Well, we can be sure of one thing. Platanus got what he was after and did what he needed to with it," Cas said.

"How do you figure that?" asked Ace.

"Simple. We live at the Fen and DragonTree's our home," Cas left the rest unsaid.

"Oh! Silly me. I should've figured that out before I asked."

"When are we going to get back, do you think?" No one was surprised that it was Mira asking that question.

"It might be soon, the rain is slackening a bit now. The mist is all gone and it's getting much brighter out there. I can see a lot more of the swamp." As Aneth was speaking, the first hints of blue sky shone through the breaking cloud cover. Sunlight was hitting the tops of the taller trees.

"See, we pretty much talked the storm away with our little history lesson," Aneth said.

"Hah, history lesson? As if you could call it that," Coria said. "We really only discovered that we never learned quite enough. Does that count as a lesson?"

"You got me there. Our history discussion lasted just long enough for the worst of the storm to pass," Aneth corrected himself. "Is that better, Coria?"

She answered him with a laugh.

Gal laughed too. "It wasn't my intention to distract everyone, but all good things work together!"

"Either way," Coria interrupted him, "that sunlight sure is a welcome sight." She sighed. Her color was bland, washed out and pale.

Everyone looked the same.

"I can feel the air heating up already. What do you say about us starting back towards home as soon as possible?" Tuss was ready to move out as quickly as they could. The idea of spending the night in such a strange place was unsettling.

"I'm with you Tuss, and I think that we might have to plan our trips out and about a little better in the future," Aneth said.

"A little better? That's an understatement, if I ever heard one," Mira said.

"There may be times we'll need to stay away overnight. Just not tonight and definitely not here," Tuss said, trying to divert them from further worrying Mira.

"Sure we will! If we go far enough, we may spend days away." Briza sounded happy about the idea. He was back to his usual, annoying self again.

"Not me, I'm not going anywhere else for ages," Mira said. "In fact, I may not be going anywhere else again. Not tomorrow and maybe not ever, not at all."

"Me either," Ace agreed. "This has been fun, well sort of fun, but I'm in no hurry to do this again. And I won't ever stay in a cold, drafty cave, not overnight."

Briza said teasingly, "But this place is so homey."

"You can go and fly straight into the dark right now for all I care, Briza," Mira shot back. "I'm most certainly done with adventures for now."

"Not yet," Briza replied with a laugh.

"Huh? Why not?"

"We're not home yet."

"I hope the fish get you on the way back," Mira's colors darkened.

A cold chill ran through Tuss at her words. *Why does that bother me so much? It must be the results of a very unusual day.*

Cas interrupted their banter, "I'll ask Auran when we get back and see what he thinks about trips that last for more than a single day. But, forget that for now, we need to get going."

"Now that's as good an idea as I've heard," Ace said.

They moved out from the cave into what was left of the daylight. Rainwater was dripping from just about everything. It sparkled as it fell through the patches of bright, late afternoon sunlight. The mist was just starting to reform on the water again, and since none of them knew exactly how long it would take to cover everything, they wanted to get going as quickly as possible. First, they needed to warm up for the long flight back.

"Look there, let's fly over to that partially sunken log, where the sun is brightest. There's plenty of room for us to perch together," Aneth said, not waiting for a reply. "And no funny business on the way back, Briza. We'll be fortunate enough to make it home before full dark. We can play around tomorrow, okay?"

"No worries, I've no intentions of playing about. There's a lot to think over and I plan on doing just that the entire way. I doubt it'll take us very long, anyway. Not if we push ourselves and fly at a steady pace."

He was almost right. It took them a little longer than expected to warm up. The breeze blowing out of the cave had cooled their blood and stiffened them more than they realized. The late day sun wasn't as warming as it was in the morning, but they were happy to have it nonetheless. They filled the wait conversing about the day. When everyone was warmed enough, they took off. They flew in a straight line south, moving confidently towards where they felt their home to be. The distance they'd traveled earlier in the day was much less than any remembered. It only took them half the evening to return to where they'd started. The game of tag was the culprit, it'd distracted them the entire journey north.

"Home," Mira said with a tired sigh as they dropped down past the last thick patch of reeds, which marked the north shore of the Fen. She flew off to her area without another word or a glance back.

The others watched her go, tired but grateful to be back. Leon followed closely behind.

Cas reminded them that she'd go and see Auran, ask their questions and find out what advice and information he could give. She told them that she'd meet them afterward and fill them in on what he had to offer. The only detail left was where they would meet. They decided that under the DragonTree was as good a place as any.

They said their goodbyes and went to their favorite perches.

When Tuss was finally alone, he tiredly reviewed the day. He couldn't quite believe that it'd only been that morning when they left. He thought about the fun they had while making their way north. He thought about the awe-inspiring size of the cliff wall, the thunderous storm, and the cave. It felt to him like it'd all happened to someone else and in some long ago time. "Well," he muttered aloud, speaking to no one in particular, "all of that may as well have been one of my daydreams."

He perched without bothering to eat. *I wonder if I'll get any sleep at all. There's so much to think about.*

A very short while later he fell asleep, dreaming of the unknown, of places unexplored and of the possibilities for new adventures.

His dreams were good ones.

Chapter Fourteen

Better Laid Plans

"Sorry Castanea, I don't have all of the answers you seek," Auran said. He hovered patiently while she related what happened the day before. Cas could tell that Auran had been anxiously waiting to hear about the journey. He was tense and more reserved than usual.

"Nothing at all? You can't tell me anything about the cave, nothing about Platanus or about why we felt so strange when we were there?" she asked in a rush.

"Slow down Cas. I said I don't have all of the answers. I didn't say that I don't have any of them. I understand your excitement and frustration, it's part of being young and curious."

"Oh! Okay then."

"First off, all I can tell you about Platanus is exactly what you already know. He traveled far and did many great deeds for the sake of DragonTree and dragonfly-kind. There was something about a cave too, and who knows what else beyond that? It could've been the same cave that you found but that would be quite a coincidence, wouldn't it?"

"Yes, almost too unbelievable to even consider. Such a coincidence would be..." Cas let the idea pass.

"But, as I mentioned before, I've not given those old stories much thought of late. There're so many rumors surrounding Platanus, flying through caves, fighting with spiders. I've likely forgotten most of the important details or mixed them up with foolish legends."

"Can you tell me who might know more?"

"You already know the answer to that one, Cas, the Elders." He expected her mood to sour, but was impressed when it didn't.

"Yeah, I figured as much. There's no one else, though?"

"No one. Our history is passed from one group of Elders to the next; it's always been that way. Sadly, much of what we knew has been lost. If an Elder perishes before passing along their knowledge to another, it's gone forever. That's why there are always three, and why they try and pool their knowledge."

"Okay. I'll ask them about Platanus. What do you know about the cliffs and what's beyond them? Briza and Coria will want the answers to those questions."

"Yes, ask them about Platanus. But as to the far north, I've never been beyond the shores of the Fen. I do know from the accounts of others that the cliffs you came to mark the end of what we know as the Fen regions. Supposedly they stretch from the DragonTree stream westward all the way to the great forest that borders the swamp. It likely goes far beyond, but that's just speculation. The truth has passed from anyone's knowledge. If you were able to fly over the crux of the cliffs, which I'd advise against, it's said that the air is much colder and eventually you would reach wide open grassy plains. It doesn't sound like a place I'd want to visit. So much of what I'm telling you is pure conjecture, though."

"It was Coria that was set on going up there. Oh! And Briza wanted to go too, and that wasn't a surprise, he's usually pretty rash like that. I thought we were going to have a real time of it, stopping them. Thankfully that big storm came along and put an end to the issue. I doubt Briza will forget about going back, though. There's something about that cave. He had the hardest time letting go. He's funny about stuff like that. There've been occasions when he doesn't seem to be all there. It's scary to see that *other* Briza. He's like a stranger, a dangerous one."

"Dangerous you say? I don't like the sound of that. Has he hurt anyone?" Auran sounded a lot like an Elder.

"Oh no! He hasn't hurt anyone. I doubt he ever would but he can be scary. And he only seems dangerous. It's as if, given the right circumstances, he would let go entirely and then who knows what'd happen? I don't want to find out."

"Maybe it'd be a good idea if you kept an eye on him?"

"We all do, Auran. I hope you don't think he's bad. I don't want you to think poorly of him. He's just a little different, is all."

"Don't worry about that my dear Castanea. But I've interrupted your story, please continue."

"Hmm, where was I," Cas had to think back a bit, "Oh yeah, it was then, after we got out of the rain that Briza, without missing a wing-beat was ready to fly straight into the cave. He doesn't seem to have many inhibitions. Maybe that's all part of that dangerous element of his."

"He's clearly a creature with strong passions, especially for mystery and adventure. If you don't watch him he may get the lot of you into trouble some day. Doubtless, he'll have the best intentions while doing so, but it'll be trouble, none the less," Auran said.

"He likes to argue with anyone about anything, and he doesn't seem to let go of an idea once it gets into his head. He's ready to try almost anything, no matter how crazy the idea might seem and we like that about him though, and he's a great friend to have. He's faithful and loyal, always willing to be there when you need him, but..." she took a breath, realizing that she was running on and on, "we just...I just worry sometimes. I hate to talk badly about him. The two of us tend to bicker a lot. I just worry. He really is a great friend."

"No harm done, Cas. It's good to be aware of the shortcomings of your companions. Being aware of who they truly are will allow you to be a better friend. Listen to me prattle on. How could dragonfly-kind know so much about concepts such as friendship? We're not supposed to court such ideas." He sounded wistful, his mind far away.

Cas looked more closely at her often strange but wise friend.

His deep laughter rumbled when he noticed her scrutiny. "I do envy the bunch of you, Cas, for your courage and your faithfulness to each other." Auran changed the subject. "I spent yesterday in long talks with the three Elders."

"Oh! How'd that go?" Cas was curious enough to forget her manners.

"It went smoothly if you must know. They took the news of your little adventure very well. They didn't act at all surprised. We even talked about those changes we keep alluding to, the ones your little cadre is responsible for."

"What'd they say about us? We haven't really done anything," Cas replied with genuine humility.

"I beg to differ," Auran said, once again laughing, "Your League, as you call it, has made a huge difference. Yesterday's adventure more than anything else convinced me of that. You must remember that I'm one of the old guard. I'm supposed to be one of those traditional types, upholding the standards and traditions and such. That includes my old friends, too. I've been spending a lot of time with them, catching up on the past, engaging in certain uhmm, activities. The more *mature* population of the Fen are watching and waiting to see what you and your *gang* are going to do next. You've become quite item of fascination these days." His voice dropped to a conspiratorial whisper, "it's all so very interesting."

"Oh my!" was all Cas could say in reply.

"Truth be told, we've decided to meet together on a regular basis, my friends and I. We even tried our own, slower version of your Capture game. It must've been a sad sight to see. I can certainly understand the appeal it holds for you youngsters, though. It's the most fun I've had in recent memory. I'm not so bored anymore. Life has become rich in ways it never was before, and that's true for all of dragonfly-kind here at DragonTree."

Cas was most surprised by the last revelation. Old dragonflies playing games? *It can't be; they're old and well...traditional. Could it really have been our little group of miscreants that's started all of this?*

"I can see that you don't quite believe me," he said.

"Uhhh, I do, or I guess I do. But aren't you a bit old for games?" She hesitated, not wanting to sound disrespectful.

"Yes, my dear, we are a bit old, but not so old that we don't want to live a little. As I said, we play a slower version. None of us wants to risk a broken wing or something worse, and don't forget that old or not, we've spent most of our time hawking and patrolling our areas. As tiresome or boring as that can be, it keeps us relatively fit and agile. We aren't as fast as we used to be, but my guess is that we could give even the best of the League's teams a reasonable challenge. Some of us old timers might have a few tricks that young Briza, Gal or even your Tuss haven't thought of. We may try out some of them in the east meadows sooner or later." He paused and sighed, "We've lived far too long by the old, lonely ways, Castanea. I'm finished with isolation and solitude."

She was happy to hear him say that many of the older dragonflies were finding joy and happiness.

"We should get back to the reasons why you came here this morning. I'm sorry that I've distracted you from your search for answers."

"Not at all," Cas said politely, "you've answered what you could. The only other thing we need to discuss would be about our group going away again, but this time it'd be for longer than a single day. What do you think about that?"

"What do I think? Hmmm," Auran's tone became very serious. He didn't answer immediately.

Cas waited patiently.

"It's not something you and your friends should enter into lightly. You must plan as best as you're able. I think you need to speak to the Elders about it as well. It's one thing to inform me that you're headed off for the day, but it's quite another to plan trips that'll last overnight or longer. The respectful thing to do would be to inform them about your intentions. They may even have some useful information for you, don't you think?"

"Yeah, they probably will. I'm not even sure that I want to go away for that long, not yet anyway. I've never spent a night anywhere other than the Fen." Cas felt she could be honest with Auran; he made her feel safe. "Should we just be content with the simple life we have? Are we being foolish by even considering it? "

"No Castanea, you're not being foolish. But it would've been if you followed Briza into the unknown. Flying over a cliff, or into a dark cave, that's foolish. I can barely believe the nerve of it. But I digress," he paused and collected his thoughts. "It's good to have doubts, to have questions. It's good that you're seeking the wisdom of others and are trying to make wiser plans."

"Okay. But, is what we're planning dangerous? Are we going too far?"

"I'd have to answer that two different ways. Yes, it's dangerous. To seek after the unknown always is. But I say no too, because you and your friends are not going to be content living every new day like the last. That much is very clear to me. Your heart's desires are ever changing. There's purpose in all of this, Tuss and I discussed that at length."

"He told me all about it."

Auran laughed, "I'm sure he did. I still don't know what that might be, but I've no doubt that there's something coming."

"I'm not so sure about what our hearts want, but I know that we're different," Cas agreed. "We've talked about it. I just hope we aren't being silly or foolish." She looked to him, hoping for more reassurance. "I hope we aren't making poor choices or getting our priorities too out-of-order."

"You're not silly or foolish. If that were the case, none of you would have flown into the swamp yesterday. That took a lot of courage, and if you were just silly young dragonflies you would've flown about the southern edge of the swamp and returned shortly thereafter, content enough. Instead, you've gone farther than any living dragonfly and returned with interesting stories to tell. Deciding together to *not* fly over the cliffs proves also that you're not foolish. As to what the right priority is, who's to say?"

"I never thought about it that way, Auran."

"Well you should have," he said. "I'd never desire to see harm come upon any of you, but I'm sure, as I said before, that there's a purpose for what's happening. I mentioned that I talked with Rumex, Salix and Gnaphalium. We chatted about the restlessness that you and our Tuss seem to have emerged with. We agree that there's something to it, something important at the core of it. We also believe that whatever that purpose may be, it's for the good of DragonTree. Even Salix has come around. That's why I'm sure you can go to the Elders and ask your questions. See what they have to offer. If there are dragonflies with knowledge about the world beyond the Fen, they'd be the ones that have it."

"You're sure they won't cause a fuss?" she asked.

"I wouldn't go that far and I promise nothing. They may fuss, quite a lot in fact, but that can't be helped. It's the job of the Elders to be concerned with the well being of DragonTree and the Fen. So if they do fuss I'm sure that it's for good reasons. Our young Coria has done a fine job of convincing them that trying to control your actions is not likely to happen either way. I believe they'll press for caution but, they'll still help you as best as they're able. What Salix has to say may even surprise you a little. He certainly surprised me yesterday."

"Well, that's settled then. I'll tell the others what you've told me. I think I may have a time convincing some of them to chat with the Elders, but I'll insist on it. I'm sure that Tuss and Aneth will back me up."

Cas and Auran said their farewells. She flew off to look for her friends under the DragonTree. She didn't have far to go, she'd been under the Trees' shadow the entire time she was talking with Auran. Cas meandered as she had much to ponder. She was learning that life could come at her faster than her young mind could keep up with. It's an unpredictable world she lived in. She was happy to be alive and able to experience it. She decided right then that it wasn't about *if* but *when* she and her friends started off on another adventure. It would be one that they planned better for. They'd have to be much more restrained along the way, more disciplined than they'd been yesterday. Going away into the unknown wasn't the time nor was it the place for games. This adventure stuff was serious business, maybe even dangerous to the point of deadly.

She was growing up. All of them were and she figured that they'd better start acting like it. They'd grown into the games in the same way, refining them as they progressed. They needed to grow into these new adventures with more thoughtful considerations. They'd gotten away with minor troubles yesterday, but that sort of *luck, do I even believe in such a concept? And if I do can it be counted on to last? That kind of 'whatever' could never last.*

The games in the meadows proved it. A well-laid plan usually ended in much better results. Relying on blind chance was a fool's choice and was apt to hurt them badly.

Cas felt contentment fill her and she felt centered. She circled back around and headed straight for the DragonTree. She was at peace, ready to face the task of planning their next journey. The last big obstacle would be to convince the stubborn among them, *who am I kidding? It's just Briza we have to contend with*, that Auran and the Elders must be informed of their plans.

Chapter Fifteen

Not So Bad

Once again, the friends found themselves listening to Cas as she told them all about her conversation with Auran. This time it was under the sweeping cover of the DragonTree. She was surprised that she wasn't being interrupted constantly, particularly when she mentioned the need to talk to the Elders.

"Wow! I didn't think this was going to go so easily," she said after finishing.

"Yeah, really. We never seem to be so, agreeable." Tuss looked directly at Briza.

"What?" Briza said innocently. He couldn't hide the sly look in his eyes. He knew what Tuss was implying.

"Nothing, Briza. Did you think I was saying that only to you? Why would you ever think that?"

Cas watched the two of them, wondering if an argument was about to erupt. She spoke before it could, "So, that's it then. Auran didn't answer all of the questions we had. But, I'm glad that we asked him. He really cares for us and told me all he knew. Next time, we should all go together. I'm sure that he'd love that."

"I will Cas, but as you say, only if all of us go. I couldn't do it alone," Mira said, "I just couldn't! You know how nervous I get."

"Yeah, but not like you used to be," Briza blurted.

191

"What?"

"I've noticed that too, Mira. You seem less nervous with each passing day. You speak up more often now and we like that."

"Thanks Tuss, that's nice of you to say." She only gave Briza a long hard look.

"Anyway, moving on," Gal said before Briza caught on.

"Yeah, Gal, the next big question." Tuss figured that he should be the one to broach this one, "who's willing to go to the Elders? All of us?"

"Yes, all of us," Gal answered. "I can't imagine why we'd do it any other way."

"That's the way of it," Briza agreed. "This will be an important meeting. Since we're planning to go on our adventures together, we should go meet with the Elders together. I haven't met Auran yet, but I trust him because Tuss and Cas do."

"All of us are going, Briza?" Mira asked.

"Sure that's the plan as far as I..." Briza's voice was sharp. Aneth cut him off.

"What the Elders say will be important. I'd like to hear what there is to hear straight from them."

"So, we're settled then?" Tuss asked.

They gave their assent.

"We just need to figure out when and where."

"This is quite the surprise, is it not?"

They were startled by an unexpected voice. It was Gnaphalium's. He, Auran and the other two Elders flew in under the canopy of the DragonTree and towards the friends. They drew near, slowed to a hover and found spots to perch upon amongst the surprised adventurers.

All nine were left momentarily speechless.

"Nothing to say for yourselves?"

They could only stare dumbfounded at Gnaphalium.

"Okay then. Speechifying is left to me. I see nine young conspirators before me; scheming and planning, trying to figure out how they can deceive the three old and foolish Elders."

"Yes, we certainly caught them." Rumex added.

They were stunned. Gnaphalium had always been friendly, showing them respect despite their youth. Tuss was sure that in his own way, Gnaphalium had been on their side, or at worst not completely against them. Maybe Cas misunderstood Auran's take on the Elder's thoughts about the young travelers.

"Caught us! What do you mean, caught us?" Briza asked loudly. He was angered by the accusation and ready for an argument. "Conspirators? Schemes? What're you accusing us of?"

"Easy, Briza, be at peace. All of you be at peace," Rumex spoke again, her voice gentle. "Gnaphalium, maybe this isn't a good time for teasing?"

Everyone looked at Gnaphalium. He was laughing.

"Laughing? You're laughing?" Cas asked.

"Please forgive an old dragonfly for having his fun. I was joking, pulling your wings if you will."

"What? You were joking?" sputtered Briza.

"Yes I was. And Rumex is right. My jesting was poorly timed, please accept my apologies. I guess the wounds from our last encounter are still too fresh, eh?"

No one wanted to answer that one.

"Alright, I'll accept the silence as consent, if not forgiveness." Gnaphalium became serious. "Allow me to get on with the business that we four have come here to conduct. My dear old friend, Auran, has been telling us about your adventures yesterday. He also mentioned that you intend to set out upon another one soon, and then possibly even more after that. Was he correct?"

"We didn't do anything wrong," Mira mumbled guiltily.

"No, my dear, I'm certain that you haven't. And I'm confident that you probably won't do so intentionally in the future. But the long term impact of your adventures is yet to be seen. With that said, we still require an answer."

Tuss spoke up, "The answer would be a definite yes. But if I understand what you've implied, it seems like you're giving us permission."

Gnaphalium's eyes brightened. "You, Tussilago show wisdom and perception beyond your age."

"Then I'm correct? You're telling us that it's okay to go?"

"Maybe yes, maybe no, or maybe I am curious to know why you've come to that conclusion."

"It's what you just said. You talked about the potential outcome of our adventures or our actions as if everything's destined to happen. So that means to me, to us, that you're implying that it's okay to continue exploring."

"What he's saying is that we understand that there's little we can do to keep you from doing pretty much whatever you desire. We know that arguing with any of you about any of this is pointless." Salix' tone was sharp, bordering on rudeness. He was looking at Coria.

Briza colored with anger. Tuss could see that fierce look in his friend's eyes. A tirade was about to follow. "YOU!" Briza began.

"No need to put it that way, Salix," Gnaphalium sounded impatient. "Calm down, Briza. You need to control that anger. Forgive us, this sort of thing is new to us, too."

"You're right Gnaphalium. My apologies." Salix didn't sound happy, but he did sound humbled.

"I guess that's good enough for me," Briza said grudgingly.

"What I was saying is that we realize that you and your friends are different. We know that, for whatever reason, you feel restless and don't have the same outlook, shall we say, as the rest of our kind."

Aneth mumbled something to himself. Tuss heard Briza whisper to Ace that *'he can say that again'*.

Cas quieted them with a very stern look.

Gnaphalium didn't miss any of it. "Ahhh yes, you prove me correct even as we speak. It's more evidence that you're different, very different. The questions we Elders have had to ask ourselves lately were not *'Should we allow this?'* Or *'What can we do to put a stop to this?'* but rather, *'Why is this?'* and *'What could it possibly mean?'*" He paused to let his words sink in and to gather his thoughts. "After our little discussion with Coria and Briza, and you know how that went." He laughed at the memory. "All of you together, ready to fly to their defense if needed. It was quite a sight to witness, dragonflies displaying unity like that. I never expected to see the day; in fact, the possibility had never even occurred to me. And once again we're back to the point I was trying to make."

"Which is?" Briza asked.

"Hush, Briza," Coria fussed. "Don't be rude."

"There has to be a reason for the group of you emerging at the same time with the same, forgive my choice of words, odd ways about you." Gnaphalium waited for an angry response, none were forthcoming. "You're special, and like it or not, we Elders can only accept how you've changed things. Imagine what it was like for us to watch as a small group of immature, newly emerged dragonflies alter almost everything we've ever known. How were we supposed to react, given our history, our habits and our ummm, proclivities as dragonflies."

"Our what?" asked Briza.

"Our proclivities, our natural tendencies, if you like," Rumex said. "You weren't paying attention during some of your classes, Briza."

"Well, yeah. I, uhhh...oh never mind." Briza had to laugh, she was right.

"We didn't mean to do anything wrong," Ace said, echoing Mira.

"We know that, Acer," said Rumex, "And that's part of why we're here now."

"Rumex is correct. Remember that we're talking about years of ingrained habits being reversed, and seemingly overnight. This has not happened before, not in any of our lifetimes. It's shocking to some, impossible for others. I even admit to being one of those who was shocked at the nerve of you. I'm happy to declare that I'm more of the mind of my friend Auran now; he's been both excited and supportive of what he's witnessed since your emergence-day."

"Yes I have. I've grown to love my new friends' eccentricities immensely," Auran sounded pleased.

Everyone looked at him, startled. Love wasn't a word often used amongst their kind.

"The Fen's certainly a different place at present. I see a new kind of community emerging from the old. It's strange and wonderful," Rumex sighed happily. "I've been of a mind with Auran, happy to see the changes from the beginning. These are exciting times. But there's reason for caution, knowing what the old stories say about periods of great change. We'd be foolish to ignore the past and what it has to tell us."

"What does it tell us? And how does it relate to our adventures?" Gal asked.

"Excellent questions, Galega. Let's allow Rumex to continue and we all may end up learning something new," Gnaphalium said.

"So, we must consider what we know of our past and consider the similarities to our current circumstances. As Gnaphalium has stated, we see a group of very special dragonflies. And, like it or not, they remind us of those from the old stories." She paused, noticing their reactions.

"You're not sure how to respond, are you?"

"No, but how could we be sure of anything?" Cas looked at the others. "I don't feel very special. Do any of you?"

"I do, sort of."

"Of course it'd be you saying that, Briza," Aneth said.

"But what does that mean?" Coria asked. She couldn't contain herself. "I for one, don't feel special either, and I certainly don't feel like I'm in a story."

"Me either," Ace added.

"Or me," said Tuss. "But, I do feel a little weird now and then. It's like I'm an outsider or I would be, if it weren't for the eight of you," he said looking at his friends. "I can't imagine what life would be like without the rest of you."

They shared knowing looks; they were more closely bound together than ever, the journey into the north had created strong connections.

"And that, Tussilago, is exactly why we're here. We know that all of you, though clearly different in your personalities and abilities, are alike in your desire for change," Gnaphalium said.

"So, we're right down to it then," Rumex stated.

"Yes, we are Rumex. We, the Elders, give you our blessings to follow your hearts. I'll go even further by strongly encouraging you to do so. My own old heart tells me more urgently with each passing day, that whatever it is that drives you is important. It may even be vital for the future of DragonTree. I feel that with my entire being. Salix, Rumex, Auran and I are all agreed."

Tuss looked at Salix, not sure if he was ready to accept everything Gnaphalium had just said.

"Yes Tussilago, even me. What I've observed since our little meeting has impressed me. And yes, it still bothers me a little, too."

Tuss watched as Salix's eyes clouded with anger.

"I hated to see the status quo of our kind, sacrificed for what I at first perceived as foolishness. But, as I've watched you and have seen how you work together, I've become impressed. I see how you so obviously want to be together and I've realized something that I was not aware of," his voice quieted, "I'm lonely, too. I live in a place that's overflowing with abundant life, but I'm alone. The realization of that, well, it's crushing. All the years of my life spent in isolation," He had to collect himself before he continued, "Watching you, I realized just how empty my life has become." He stopped, choked with emotion.

No one spoke. This was not the Salix they were used to.

Gnaphalium finally broke the silence, "We better move this meeting forward. We need to talk about the old stories. Those you were told when you were young nymphs. What I assume you know by now is that the stories you were told, while completely true were not truly complete."

"I knew it!" Briza shouted. "They always seemed to have gaps and missing bits."

"It was decided generations ago to limit what is told to the young; it was believed that giving too much information too early does more harm than good." Salix had regained his composure.

"We can still debate the logic of that belief," Rumex said. "There's both good and bad in limiting knowledge. We'd hate to be responsible for stealing the innocence from our young, so we erred in favor of caution."

"Please understand, though," Gnaphalium continued, "that we'll tell you what we know and will answer your questions as best we can. The stories are old and so much has been lost over so many generations. I promise that we won't hold anything back."

"That's not so bad though," said Tuss.

"How's that not a bad thing, Tuss?"

"Not knowing everything is okay, Briza. It leaves a lot of mysteries open for us to discover on our own."

"Well I guess that makes a lot of sense, although..."

"I'm with Tuss on that," Cas interrupted Briza, "but I do want to hear the story of Platanus. Isn't that what you were about to tell us?" Cas looked at the Elders, expecting them to begin telling them a more complete history than they'd heard before.

"Yes, Castanea. But, we're called Elders for a reason and we tire out much sooner than the lot of you. It'll take more energy than I have left this afternoon to tell what I know. Don't you agree?" Gnaphalium was asking Rumex and Salix the question. Not surprisingly, both agreed.

The meeting was over.

***

"That wasn't so bad," Cas said.

Tuss didn't answer her. They were flying back to the north end of the Fen.

"Typical! Always lost in his thoughts, is my Tuss."

"Huh?" he said. The tone in her voice was what got his attention. "What were you saying, Cas?"

"I was saying that it wasn't so bad, meeting with the Elders like that. You haven't heard a thing I've said, have you?"

"I guess I haven't and don't look at me like that. I was thinking about the first meeting we had under the DragonTree. This one was sort of similar"

"Similar? Really? How?"

"Everything back then was fresh and exciting, you remember that, right?"

"Yeah I do," She replied.

"We were newly emerged and naive about life above. We met under the Tree, talked a lot and when we were finished, I took the time to actually look around at the amazing beauty of this place."

"Go on," she said.

"Alright. So, I remembered looking about, realizing how amazing the world was. It filled me with an overwhelming sense of wonder about everything. Do you remember feeling that, too? I hope you do, because right now I feel like I'm not making a whole lot of sense here."

"You're making perfect sense. Back then, everyday life was an adventure. We didn't know what to expect, but we knew that we were going to face it together. It was just the nine of us."

"Yeah, that's right, just the nine of us. It wasn't long before nine became fifty then fifty became a hundred," Tuss said.

"Now, it's the nine of us again, or maybe nine. I'm not so sure that Ace and Mira will join us when we go off again, especially if we plan to stay away overnight. It probably depends on what the Elders tell us. Who knows?" As she spoke Tuss had to fight not to laugh. She sounded just like him right then, lost in thoughts, a daydreamer. He stayed silent not wanting to interrupt her. He loved watching her work through things. He'd happily spend the rest of the evening, probably the rest of his life staring into her eyes and listening to her talk. A sound finally escaped him, half laugh, and half sigh.

"What was that?" she snapped out of the reverie. "What are you laughing at?"

"You, I'm laughing at you. You remind me of me."

"Oh, I do? That's not good." She sounded serious. "Two of you, I shudder to think of it."

"So, you're saying that it doesn't work for you? Us being alike, it's a problem?" he asked impishly.

"It would be if true. But it isn't, so it's not. AND, I'm not absent-minded."

"Ouch!" Tuss acted like he was hurt. "You're worse than Briza."

"So, where were we?" she asked, ignoring the insult.

"The nine of us. The meeting and so forth. The nine of us today, just like last time."

"Yeah. So, we're looking forward to the unknown once again. It's exciting and new, and we'll face it together. Who knows what we'll see or what we'll do. Is that what you meant?" Cas asked.

"I can hardly remember what I meant. But what you just said, that's about as good as I could put it. So, yes, it was a lot like our first meeting."

"See! Nothing like you. I make sense," she teased.

"Maybe, but that's just your opinion. In the end though, alike or not, life's looking like it's going to be very exciting for us again." He chose then to change the subject, "Are you hungry?"

"I sure am," she answered. Tuss saw a funny shine in her eyes. It was something that hadn't been there before.

"What?" he asked

"Huh?"

"What is it?" he asked again.

"What is what? You asked me about heading off to hawk and I said yes."

"Yeah, but that look," He paused hoping that she'd say something. When she didn't he said, "Oh, never mind, I'm so hungry, I don't know what I'm saying."

"No doubt," she replied.

"What?" he asked again, but she was off chasing the evening's meal.

***

"That wasn't so bad, was it?" he said, once they'd eaten their fill.

"Ha! That's what I said before!"

"You? When? Just now?" He was confused.

"Right after the Elders and Auran left, just before I dragged you out of your thoughts and back into reality again. I was saying that the meeting..."

"What about it?"

"I was saying that the meeting wasn't so bad. It was nothing like I expected it'd be."

"But I was the one that just said that." He was even more confused.

Cas snickered, "Oh, never mind! It's getting dark, let's head home and get some rest."

They spent that night closer to each other than ever before. Tuss was perched in a new place, well within sight of Cas' favorite spot. It was a natural reaction to the new intimacy they shared. He liked seeing her as sleep began to overtake him.

Tomorrow, he thought, *yeah, tomorrow's going to be very interesting.*

Chapter Sixteen

From Another Perspective

Idalia the butterfly was more troubled now than ever before. She knew that she was the only butterfly that would be. She'd spent all of yesterday near the massive tree the silly creatures referred to as the DragonTree. She thought back over how things had gone. The memories were very clear and they would not stop running through her busy mind...

***

It was an unusual day, which began when Idalia woke from the long restless sleep. Throughout the night she'd dreamed of one particular location, she knew the place well. It was a nice little patch full of wildflowers that grew on the west side of the Fen. She knew that she would go there, though it was a long flight and the journey would take her further south than she cared to travel. It was that or cross over the open expanse of water again, which wasn't a sensible option. She'd done it before and derided herself for days after. But distance and danger aside, all she could think of was how nice it would be to spend a peaceful day, far away from the noisy dragonflies that so often filled the east meadows, busy in their chaotic activities. She knew that strange events were happening around the Fen. The dragonflies were breaking

203

from their normal behavior. They were flying everywhere in groups and that was something they'd never done before. They were acting very strangely; the ridiculous games were the most obvious and bothersome of the changes. The overall results were that the normal rhythms of life were affected for all of the creatures living near the Fen, the butterflies more so than others. Their once peaceful browsing grounds were constantly disturbed by the riot of undignified activity.

Idalia knew that the meadows didn't belong to any specific kind of creature, but for generations it was the butterflies that spent most of their waking time therein. She'd concluded from many days of observations that the east meadows would never be the same. The peace she and her kind were used to was gone for good. But angry as she was, Idalia still wondered about the timing of these recent events. It couldn't just be coincidence that the nine young dragonflies began the silliness just when the foreign bees, large, strange and dangerous looking had arrived. *Could it really be that, so to say?*

She wasn't sure, but it seemed to Idalia that it was the very same day when she'd first overheard the young dragonflies plotting their new lives and she'd first noticed the bees.

"Oh well! There's nothing to be done at this moment, so to say." She sighed deeply and resigned herself to the day ahead. She looked about, making sure that no one had heard her vocalize which wasn't proper behavior this early in the morning, she would be accused of being as noisy as the interloping dragonflies.

No matter what happens tomorrow or the day after, I still have today and it's a lovely day, the perfect time for me to fly over to the west meadow. And just like that Idalia went, completely forgetting her concerns and hesitations. The sun was high and bright in the blue sky; so warm and lovely. It was the kind of day she could get lost in, spending her time fluttering from flower to flower, enjoying everything she saw, "everything but those loud creatures, I must say!"

And so, there she found herself, out over the smooth, mirror surface of the Fen. *Amazing! Simply, amazing!* Idalia was looking at her reflection. Her colors glowed. She was orange, black and white, with multicolored spots running along the edges of her wings. Her body was striped all along its length. She never tired of looking at herself. Her friend, Nokomis, was just as lovely, but only when looking down at the watery mirror was she able to fully appreciate what she looked like to him.

Soon enough her reflection vanished; mud, rocks and greenery replaced it. She was across the Fen. She'd made it safely to the western shore. *Good, that's a relief. Flying across the water is dangerous business. I'm glad that I'm finished with it for now. I shouldn't have done that again. I should've gone around following the southern shore. I wonder why I didn't?*

Idalia berated herself; full of disbelief at the risk she'd taken. *What was I thinking?* And that was the problem. She realized that she hadn't been thinking at all or else she wouldn't have chanced it. She'd be more careful in the future. *But I can't shake the feeling that I was drawn here by something more.*

She felt the western breeze buffet her. The strong fragrance of the big tree filled her senses as she flew around the widely spreading branches. She was careful to leave plenty of space between her wings and those sappy green needles. One brush against the wrong limb would be the end of her. Tree sap was dangerous and nasty. A few quick wing-beats and she was past the entanglement. *Ahhh, now that's much better.* She was surrounded by flowers that bloomed in great bunches. They were of every color and every variety and she had them all to herself. *Oh wonderful!*

This little stretch of open space between the water and the eastern forest was filled with more flowers than she could count. She was sure that this abundance of loveliness was why she was drawn to this place and not some crazy middle-of-the-night dream. It had to be something simple like that, even though she...

"What? You're joking!"

Idalia was familiar with the voice. It was that silly, vain dragonfly, one she'd seen far too often. He was one of the original troublemakers. She could hear all of them underneath the tree, talking. She was reminded again of the first time she'd taken notice of them. It was not so long ago, several full moons had passed but not many days more. There were others there with them this time, though. From the way they sounded she guessed that they were older dragonflies. She could hear them discussing many things as she browsed the flowers of the meadow. She could understand very little of what they were saying but she listened intently anyway.

Is this why I came here today? Am I supposed to observe something? Was there a purpose to be found in that crazy dream? Maybe it wasn't the flowers that had drawn Idalia; maybe it was the need to hear more about what the silly dragonflies were up to. She'd been nervous lately and hoped to find some way to relieve herself of the burdens and concerns, if possible. She wondered if listening would bring more understanding or maybe, more trouble.

She wrestled with her doubts, beat them back, stilled her mind and finally was able to relax. At peace once more, she gave her full attention to what was being said. It went on and on.

***

Idalia woke from her daydream as the memories from yesterday faded away. There was no need to recall every detail of the conversation. It would stay in her mind, stored away until she needed to remember. Idalia sometimes wished it was possible for her to forget the things that would make life a lot less troubling.

Her problem was that she saw too much, and that meant that she remembered too much, which in turn forced Idalia to think too much. *My head hurts and my heart is heavy. I'm worried and there's no one I can share with, no one except for Nokomis.*

She was feeling very strange. She knew that bad creatures had come to the Fen and she knew of their unusual interest in the nine dragonflies. She had watched them watch the nine. She couldn't forget about it and she couldn't stop thinking that it had become her responsibility somehow. Did her unwanted knowledge of what had happened, or might happen, require her to help the neighbors that she and her kind shared this part of the world with? She was sure that Nokomis would say *No*. He was very committed to the butterfly Creed. Their purpose was to observe and remember and not interfere. It made no sense to Idalia, this whole idea of being part of this world, and yet choosing to have nothing to do with it. She knew that she could positively affect it and it's other inhabitants without the worst of it affecting her negatively. But if she didn't or wouldn't even try, well, she knew what hypocrisy was and hated it most when she found it in herself. *Why am I so different and why can't Nokomis be different, too?*

Was it only two days ago that she'd asked herself, *'If I...No, if we see something wrong and do nothing about it, what does that say about us?'*

And there it was, the core of her worry, impossible to ignore. Something was happening at the Fen and she knew that it meant trouble. The strange bees did not belong. She instinctively felt how wrong they were when they were nearby. There was a kind of sickness about them. They triggered her sense of danger. She felt waves of something pulsing from them. Was it evil? Their very presence was like a blight that affected the air itself. *Just how much trouble do they represent and what am I supposed to do about it?* Idalia was certain that if circumstances became bad, she and her kind would simply move on to a safer location in some other region. *And that's all we'd do. Just go away and leave the other creatures to their fate. What is fate anyway?*

The butterflies would move to wherever seemed safe and then return to their old habits. She hated the idea. She couldn't picture herself living contentedly that way, simply because she wasn't that kind of creature. For whatever reason, Idalia was born to be different. The time had come for her to change; she could feel it. Even if it meant acting alone, she needed the peace that action would bring. She felt the truth, and knew in her heart of hearts that the Creed was in agreement. She would comply with what her heart demanded of her.

Consequences? Will there be consequences? Her fellow butterflies would rebuke her for interfering, but that didn't matter. She could use their own Creed as a defense, tell them not to interfere with her, just observe. She laughed at the thought of it, recognizing for the first time that the Creed was all encompassing like that. There was so much to it. Idalia knew her mind would never be able to wrap itself around all the truth their beliefs held. She found comfort in seeing her limitations and finding something that was much bigger than she was. *So yes, there'll be consequences, but what might occur if I don't?*

She'd come to believe that the consequences of not telling the dragonflies, the only creatures that might be able to deal with the dangerous invaders, were probably far worse. They were silly and noisy and innocent in their own way. Better yet, they were fierce and deadly as well. Hadn't she observed the almost unrestrained power they demonstrated as they played their games? If they were warned, if they knew, maybe they could do something. There weren't any others. *So then, if interfere I must, why not here and now?*

Her heart filled with resolve. The others would call her rebellious and troublesome. But so what? If she followed her heart as it now led, she wouldn't care what they thought or said. Idalia felt better knowing that she'd do what she believed was right, finally acting on her deepest inclinations. *Yes, I'm different and yes, my kind's Creed has always worked well in the past, but from the past I must learn.*

Butterflies were always so passive about everything. *But not me, not any longer, I need to break from the old way of thinking and grow.*

She asked herself once again, only this time in a more personal fashion, *'If I see something wrong and do nothing about it, what does that say about me?'*

It was time to interfere.

Idalia would approach the dragonflies and tell them of her observations. She'd warn them about her fears and concerns. She would, for the first time in her life, directly interact with creatures of another kind. There was no question about which one she'd approach; the loud and vain one. From her observations, he'd be the easiest to appeal to. She only hoped that she could communicate her concerns clearly and that he'd believe her. *I wonder where all of this will lead?*

Chapter Seventeen

Yet Another Perspective

The time for the invasion had come. The last of the scouts and spies returned, their missions accomplished. They were once again together within the confines of Hive. The group-mind was whole. The Queen's Imperative for conquest could move forward. Only Third and her ambushers would execute otherwise. They were in the west and would remain there until their mission was accomplished.

All was ready but the Queen was silent. The group-mind looped back upon itself, the Imperative implanted recycled the message, *We are Hive...We will conquer...*But only after the Queen regained consciousness. Until then, the bees of Hive acted like any other bees.

Epilogue

What Tomorrow May Bring

Tuss and friends spent an interesting if not anxious night, waiting to see what revelations would come to light on the morrow. They would gather with their good friend Aurantium and the three Elders. All of them knew that no matter what twists and turns the meeting and all that followed took, they'd face it together. They'd grown into something more than they could easily define. They were bound by nature, singular in purpose and yet separate individuals. They loved each other and had enough shared experiences to bind them in heart and mind.

Cas stated it simply, "we're undeniably curious to many, maybe odd to some, but most importantly a singular body, formed from diverse parts."

Tomorrow would be the day when the rest of their lives, surely not destined to be mundane, but rather filled with discovery and adventure, would truly begin.

***

Idalia, fully aware of the impact her next actions might have in her life, but absolutely determined to do what was right, passed that night peacefully. Her resolve wouldn't waver. She'd chosen to spread her wings just a bit wider than she'd ever done before. Once that conscious

211

decision to grow beyond her comfortable, known world was made, illogically, her heart found the rest and peace it needed to face anything the horizon brought to her.

***

The minions of Hive only waited for the Queen's command. When it finally came they would swarm into the west following the Imperative's ceaseless pulsing beat, We are Hive...We are Legion...We shall conquer...

The End

Contact Shon at dragontreeonline@protonmail.com

Continued in:

DragonTree
The Battle for DragonTree

Made in the USA
Middletown, DE
18 December 2021

54209133R00119